D1274149

ARMADILLO IN THE GRASS

ARMADILLO
IN
THE
GRASS

SHELBY
HEARON

ALFRED A. KNOPF

NEW YORK 1968

TO ANNE AND REED

ARMADILLO IN THE GRASS

CHAPTER

EVERY morning fat Clyde, my cat, and I come to the edge of our woods with my first cup of hot coffee. As I drink Clyde digs in the sumac leaves under the live oaks, making his bathroom. This part of the woods is the territory of the mockingbirds who shout at us and at a cross bluejay who also comes each morning to fuss at Clyde.

Today as the jay dives at the cat's head and the mockers chase the jay, I watch the daylight crawl into the cold ravine below the woods. A dry biting wind, carrying the smell of thawed cedar, makes me pull my bare feet under the heavy coat that covers my thin gown.

It is the sixth day of a new year and I am trying to

make a resolution about twenty-five pounds of clay which Anslow, my husband, has brought me to work with. He has just had published a book on the Middle Ages, his specialty at the college here where he teaches, a book he has labored over a long time. The clay, I think, is his way of trying to help me with a problem the book has reminded me of: that we do not see the world the same way.

He has worked his chapters with care to show the slow process by which, step by step, under the security of medieval institutional rigidity, technological change pyramided the world into modern times. As he says, he intends to leave the suggestion that we are once again on the threshold of such expansion.

It is hard for me to see the world as a series of inter-connected events like that. It is harder for me to understand why this carefully worked out idea about the machines beside the castles has so much more value to him now that it is in print. It is almost as if he cared more about the evidence of his work than about the work itself.

I see the world in pictures.

Yesterday was typical of this difference between us. When Anslow came home, loping across the yard with the new book in his hands, I was on my hands and knees talking down a tunnel to the retreating back of an armadillo.

I have a picture of an armadillo that makes me welcome each one that pits our yard. The picture is of a female (perhaps the great-great-grandmother of this one) who left South America's lush larvae-hung roots, to crawl under a bony back up the length of mountainous Mexico across the muddy Rio Grande, to make a nest under the baking Texas sun for her four identical babies. For that armadillo—archaic, toothless, slow, encased in a thin armor of small bony plates—it was a long trip.

Anslow whistled as he came across the yard. His fair face was flushed up to his receding hairline. It was good to see him so pleased.

"The first copy!" He waved a thick volume down at me.

I jumped up and threw my arms around his chest.

He asked, "You still talking to that wetback?"

"Yes. It is so dry I don't see how she lives." I dug dirt from under my fingernails. "Let me wash my hands. I want to see the book—"

Later we sat in the library as darkness swallowed our woods and bourbon made a nest in my stomach and I carefully handled the book. I told him that I was very proud.

This pleased him and he went to get me something from the car. It was a heavy plastic-wrapped sack from the ceramic shop. "This is a thank you for putting up with all the proofreading."

"You didn't need to." But it felt good in my hands and I remembered aloud, "You got me some before."

He smiled. "I keep trying to get you to translate

some of the time and concern you spend on the ground with your animals into something we can all share."

This was part of an old discussion we had had before. "You just don't think anything exists except when you can show it to someone else."

"If *I* wandered around in the middle of the night feeding scraps to half the four-legged animals in the state, I'd want some proof of my sanity." He laughed in his way that reminded me that it was a bad time for an old fight.

So I told him I would work the clay, and admired the typeface in his book.

He does not understand that it is enough for me to sit in the damp grass in the dark nights through the speeding years because I know who I am when I sit there: I am Clara Blue who hates the raccoon and loves the possum.

My picture of raccoons is of the two that wait by the feeder trays at night. The first pair that came eight years ago woke me by shaking the lids off the garbage cans. They were small, with ragged coats, and ravenous. Standing on hind legs they sucked at cans and jars like bear cubs. It was one thing to know from school that they were a cousin of the bear, that they had plantigrade feet and were omnivorous and were even a distant cousin of ours.

But it was another to see them sucking and shoving like caricatures of bears in the moonlight. Unlike the bear, who has no facial muscles to show his reactions, the raccoon, as he glances over his shoulder, peers at your face, and grabs for his food, carries on with what appears to be a constant desire to please. It is this willingness to compromise that makes him much less, for me, than the bear.

I see the very first mammal, our common ancestor, perched in a tree trying to survive. It is as if her evolutionary children all tried a different method: the bear came down, heavy and fur-coated, out of the trees to try to make it on brute strength alone; the ape stayed in the tree and swung his way out of danger; our grandmother crept down, bare, using her wits to look for tools; but the raccoon tried to play all the angles and is still in and out of trees and feeder trays ready to go along with everybody.

The current pair, fat and overfed, bark crossly on hind legs when I am late, or climb the pecan tree outside my bedroom and shake its branches against the window until I come. Watching them I get uneasy that they may be so adaptable they'll be around sucking honeycombs and crawdad shells when we and the bears are fossils under their flat feet.

But the possum I love. She, like humans, sees poorly, hears badly, moves slowly, and eats messily. She has no defenses except to slow down her breathing and play dead. I have seen dogs sniff at a still possum, who must somehow keep any odor from its breath, and turn away embarrassed as if they had been fool enough to smell a couch cushion.

I see her as she looks coming cautiously to eat what the raccoons leave. She blinks constantly over her shoulder, picking at remains with long teeth and bare black fingers. She steps in the water pan, trips over bread crusts, searching for the juicy cantaloupe or grapefruit rinds which are her favorite.

She goes along unaware of the genetic miracle of opposable thumbs which are stuck on her back feet, living only until her thirteen babies, small enough when born to fit into a teaspoon, can fend without her. It is a grim way to survive—foraging on leftovers with babies clinging to your back—but my defenseless friend the possum has survived, while other species died out, through more centuries than I can imagine. I respect her defenseless tenacity and love to watch her eat.

But explaining this to Anslow is not easy for me. It may not be any easier to show him with the clay.

I don't know if he got the clay because he wants to see how I picture the animals, or if he wants me to have something to show the way he has his book. Maybe he doesn't know himself.

Maybe he remembers that the other times I worked with clay were nice times. I was doing some modeling when we met, was deep in a crisis at the zoology building, trying to flesh the lifeless forms in comparative anatomy out into living shapes. Then three years ago, when the boys were small—in fact, Cal was just a baby —Anslow got me some clay after we had seen some ancient Indian cave drawings out West.

Clyde jumps in my lap, spilling the last of the coffee on my legs, to tell me it is time for breakfast. I grab him like a ball of clay—pushing, pulling, rolling him until he bites my wrist with his domesticated jaws.

"You're a marshmallow, Clyde," I tell him.

CHAPTER

WITH a fresh cup of coffee I get Anslow and the boys ready to leave.

Arch, my eight-year-old, who was named for his father, Archer Anslow Blue, has trouble finding his homework, a sheet of paper full of pluses and minuses. We find it under his bed stuck to a discarded piece of chewing gum.

Cal, named George Callison Blue, after my father, spills his eggs and says, "Bad Mama," because I have set the plate too close. When he is mad he makes fists and closes his eyes and is an intractable three-year-old.

Anslow looks scrubbed and has the air of a man who is published. He keeps an arm around my shoulders while he plans a celebration party. "Not a large crowd.

Let's make it dinner. Do you feel up to a real dinner?"

"Anything." I smile up at him.

He savors that.

"Who do you want?"

He considers. "Hayes and Sarah of course. But nobody else from school. Maybe the couple who had us over before Christmas, Evan and Louise."

"The lawyer."

"Yes." He smooths his thinning hair. "Let me think about it. Not a large crowd." After a minute he says with feeling, "I wish your father were here, Clara."

I ask, "Did you send him a copy?"

"They sent him one straight from the press. He had, you remember, extracted a promise from me for the first copy."

I tell him, which is true, "He thinks a lot of you, An."

"With all he's done that's very kind. I asked in the note I sent him for a little more detail on his current project on schizophrenia."

I laugh. "He's probably off on something else by now."

He sighs. "Clara, you can sound so much like your mother. I'll never figure how those two people got together: your father, with all his significant work in biochemistry, and your mother, who sits in their garden, unimpressed with his work."

He has captured the exact picture of my parents that I always carry in my head. They sit in the garden—

wherever they are there is always a garden—which my father likes to call his solar system, because he has something always blooming, something always dying.

He is working with pigmented hands, and no shirt, in the dirt. In front of him are open cloud-clusters of orange bougainvillaea, around him are scattered white dwarf roses and giant reds and yellows, behind him is a vast nebula of ranuncula and calendula. He is immersed in his ever-expanding universe.

My mother, a stillness in the center of the garden, meditating in long-practiced oriental style, wears a calm translucent freckled face and a wreath of braids.

They are both caught in the oriental fragrance of a galaxy of flowers: they are both living in the present moment.

I throw my arms around Anslow's chest in fierce delight at the picture of my family.

He is puzzled. "Now why did that please you? You are a funny girl. I never know how you'll take something."

Arch tugs on his sleeve, "Come on, Dad, we'll be late."

And Cal shouts at me that Clyde is eating his eggs off the floor and that it is my fault.

It is not Cal's nursery day, so I put him in the back yard with a bucket and spoons in the sandpile and he and the cat both begin to dig in the sand.

After another cup and the beds and dishes there is nothing between me and getting started on the clay.

It has been a long time and my hands are awkward. I am self-conscious with it, watching anxiously to see if I am handling it well. In school I had the picture of a bone structure in my mind and had only to flesh it out with my hands.

I try to put my mind on the raccoon who comes to feed. But I have forgotten, forgotten how to get an image from my mind down into my moving hands. The clay seems too dry and I get a bowl of water to wet my hands in. It begins to move under the pressure of my fingers.

Roughly I shape a raccoon with an arched back and all four feet on the ground. But as I round it out it lumbers at me like a trained bear. I move the lines and make thin "hands," a more pointed head. That is better, but the tail looks as if it belongs to a squirrel.

Although I concentrate on the raccoon that I hate in precise detail, my hands continue to translate it into clumsy copies. It must be like this for a baby who sees what walking and eating are about but who cannot send the right messages to his legs or hands, or from his hands to his mouth. It is very frustrating.

Cal, who sits outside patting in the sand, does not

have this trouble; he is not thinking about doing a tunnel in the sand, he is just doing it with total concentration. It is me who is somehow in the way between my mind and my hands.

With wet hands I wipe my hair off my cheeks and stand back to look at it. The head juts out of the shoulders at a plane higher than the tail—this is right. The jaw, which I have shifted several times, curves in to meet the angle where the slender feet reach forward. That looks right. For an hour or more I work it: work the legs farther apart in the back, work the head back and then down, move the front paws closer together. Exhausted from being moved so much, it falls off balance onto its face.

I press muddy hands to my cheeks. The worst is that the more I get it to look like a raccoon—that is, the more recognizable it becomes—the more it looks like any raccoon and the less it shows of my particular visitor. The more exact I get it, the less it reveals.

This time I put about half the clay, about twelve pounds, up into a rough standing position. I try to rough out quickly a suggestion of a beggar by the feeder pans. I am wetting it and turning it when Cal comes in.

"Do we have any apples or cookies or anything?" he asks, coming up to stare at what I am doing.

"Apples. I am trying to make a raccoon. Can you tell?"

"No. It doesn't look like much of a raccoon to me. I bet I can do it." He reaches sandy hands for the clay.

"Sure, go ahead." I tell him. He is so sure of himself I have to smile.

He hammers down on the clay until it is a bulge patted down flat onto the kitchen table. Wiping his hands on his pants he goes to look for an apple.

The bulge is of course better than what I was doing.

Grateful for the lesson I get a strong cup of coffee and begin to pat the clay.

CHAPTER

{ 3 }

MOCKINGBIRDS are out scissoring gray on white tails as thin snowflakes layer our path of limestone flakes called caliche. Clyde chases the wet snow, becoming abused when it melts on his bare nose. Fat and black, he looks sweet against the white cover on the gray path.

Yellow jonquils edge the woods on spring-green stalks, crimson redbud blooms burst out on bare limbs. The mockers and I shout back and forth; the coffee is scalding. It is a good picture for a cold dawn.

If a groundhog lived in Texas he could see his shadow today splashed against the spread of snow.

If he lived here I would probably be ramming my thick head against the wall trying to make his likeness in clay, as frustration has become my daily medium.

There is a wild dream I have in which all the crippled, distorted, bizarre raccoons I have made during this long month take over the world: the world crawls from sea to sea with masked mistakes begging for food. It is a bad dream which is too close to the reality of my mornings.

Everyone has tried to help.

Anslow, who said perhaps it wouldn't be *giving up* for me to try drawing instead, gave me a box of charcoals.

My friend Sarah tried to sign me up for a ceramic class at the museum school.

Arch thinks my attempts are grand: he took one for Show-and-Tell.

Cal adores the clay and half the mornings he works with me: completely relaxed, talking constantly, and making better shapes than mine with his smaller stubby hands.

Mother sent a longer letter than usual which was intended to speak to my condition:

> Michigan's snow is an obstacle your father enjoys. His plants are in the glassed-in porch which it pleases him to call the Greenhouse.
>
> The urinary-patter studies are not making the results he expected. This elates him considerably as does the depression of his colleagues. So this is a good winter for him.
>
> Don't send any more pictures of the boys. I hold them

as immobile as the snapshot until the next one arrives. It is a jerky way to watch my grandsons grow.

If your clay work had come easily it would not be what you want. You are working at it too directly. Become the raccoon. *You are the rabbit in the grass; he is also the grass.*

Love,
Mother

P.S. The wives here, as I told you, dress very practically.

That last meant that her freckled face was lonely among the faculty wives. That problem runs in the family.

However, her rabbits in the grass were no better than the charcoals and classes and being loved in the second grade. What I need is a teacher, and I think I found him yesterday.

I went on one of those museum visits where you take prospective faculty wives so they can see what a cultural place this would be to live. We were all in what Mother would call practical clothes: bandaged against the fresh scab of snow on the concrete walks. The visiting girls—young and Yankee—had pastel coats to show that they were in fashion. Their hair was done in something Sarah called a beehive style. Sarah, dressed in a brown suit, was in charge of the tour.

The museum smelled of central heat and air: faintly

metallic and enclosed. The large movable flats were hung with stylized tapestries. The main room (incandescent with blue daylight pouring in from northern skylights) had an unexpectedly happy collection of large oils, matted and abstract, that blurred up close into a mass of brushstroke and sun-streaked colors. From across the room you realized that these were myopic visions of river banks and meadows, seen too close for the eye to focus.

"Very nice!" I said out loud to the pictures.

While the pastel girls and the brown girls were discussing in a common language the meaning of modern art, over against the glass wall that looked out on a sloping lawn littered with cold students I saw five welded pieces on wood pedestals.

Two of the pieces, birds, made a hard knot in my stomach. The large bird flapped its interminable pointed wings so loud my head swam; the smaller bird stood on one foot, staring with one protruding eye—he had no beak. They were very male, very bird, but very individual. I knew them, in fact recognized them, as if they were birds that lived under the live oaks. The name on the figures said Locke Smith.

Here was my teacher.

The girls stayed for a tour and coffee.

As I left with Mr. Smith's name, I heard an artist complain to a student: "You spend six months working your fingers numb tilting the colors down a plane, just so, then a lady walks by and says, 'Very nice.' It's enough to make you quit."

Impatient with me for staying too long by the yellow flowers, fat Clyde rubs up against me like a wet seal to remind me it is time for breakfast.

While we eat Anslow reads the paper. He starts each day with what it says. I do not understand newspapers because they have nothing about the present; they are promises about the future based on guesses about the past.

After breakfast I remind him, out in the cold by the car, "Don't forget. Sarah and Hayes are coming for supper."

He puts his arm around my shoulder. "You already reminded me. You have reminded me twice. You're jumpy this morning. Something on your mind?"

"Those birds I saw."

"You were going to call that sculptor."

I hesitate. This is difficult for me. "Is it all right about the money for lessons? If he'll take me."

"Don't worry about that."

"You always say that when I ask for things, but I have a problem about asking."

He sighs. "I know."

"Will you get something in from the book?"

He is impatient. "I said don't *worry* about it." He stands a minute and then says, "Go ahead and call him."

Arch calls, "Come on, Dad, we'll be late." He has his lunch money, his overdue library books, his recopied spelling papers, and a brief kiss for his mother. He is long and fair like his father, with the same elegant tapered head, wide at the crown, narrow at the jaw. Until his great smile breaks it up into only Arch you can see where the tangle of yellow hair will in thirty years recede, where the skin across the cheekbones will sag.

He tugs at Anslow's sleeve and gives me the smile and says, "See you," in the way that reminds me he is going to see his friend Jeb after school.

After they have gone Cal goes through the ritual that precedes his two mornings at nursery school.

"Tell Miss May hello," I say.

"I like Miss May. She doesn't make me pick up everything any more."

"And Patty and Lisa and Debbie."

"They're girls."

"And Mike and David."

"They're making a road with Lee and me that we get to walk on if it rains. We're making a road out of all that sand and Miss May gave them some rocks but we're going to get some too and—"

He is interrupted by the horn out front. "There's Lee!" he says, racing off.

"Lee! Hey, I'm coming!" His wide barrel chest is crammed into an old coat, his stubby legs poke the ground as he runs. His hands (off to dig in sand, fifty years away from pigmented spots) wave at his true-blue friend who waits at the car window sucking his thumb in anticipation.

CHAPTER

{ 4 }

I DO the dishes and make the beds before I call him. I even wash out some socks for the boys.

I am scared that his name won't be in the telephone book; that it isn't Locke Smith at all but is probably Claude Abbott with two *t*s; that he lives with an old blind mother and that the telephone is in her name; or with a roommate who raises goshawks and the listing is in his name . . .

But it *is* in the phone book. Probably his wife will answer. How do I ask for him? There must be a pad by the receiver with a schedule of the lessons he gives.

It rings seven times before a man's voice says, "Yes?"

"I—I want to make a raccoon."

There is a dry laugh. "Say, you *do* have a problem."

I try again. "I saw your birds and—"

"Those damn things are always getting loose."

I stared at the phone.

He says, "You still there?"

"Yes."

"Sorry. You caught me by surprise with that opener."

"Do you give lessons was what I wanted to ask."

"Only to eat. Only as often as I have to to eat. Judas, there is every kind of class you can dream up."

"No class. I have twenty-five pounds of clay and for one month I've been trying to—"

"Right. It's coming clear. You going to enter it somewhere or something?"

I take a deep breath and retort, "In a fat-stock show."

He laughs. "I deserved that. So bring that coon in."

"When?"

"How about right now? Any excuse to put off this thing I'm working on. Besides, I'm going to set the price so high you might as well get instant service."

Without answering I hang up the phone and wrap my bundle in a damp towel. It takes fifteen minutes to find the street listed in the book, fifteen more to find the door on what must once have been a carriage house.

A small bony man with close-cut hair comes to the door. He has on jeans and tennis shoes, as I notice I do also.

He stares at me. "You're not a culturette after all, are you?"

Having no answer for that I just stand there.

"Name?"

"Clara Blue."

"Smuggle him over here in his plain wrapper, Clara Blue."

He leads me to a rough table where we stand in the strong daylight from a row of high windows on the north wall.

He unwraps the clay carelessly, asking, "Where is he?"

"I smashed the last one I did."

"So start again."

Terrified, I grab two hands full, put the shape down on all fours. Without looking up, very self-conscious as he is standing coughing at my elbow, I rough in a head, legs, haunches. A small beggar grows toward me, looking around for food, looking ludicrous.

After a while he reaches over and rolls the clay into a ball.

"Come over here, Clara Blue."

We stand before an unpainted wooden table. The room smells of oil fields, although I don't yet know why. Flecks of dust float on the rays of light coming down on the table. There are two welded women, sort of idly dumped on top of what looks like a piece of canvas.

They are painfully good.

"See these girls? You've got to understand what makes them different from each other. First you have to understand every goddam thing about your particular girl, see? Think like she thinks, waddle like she does, have a craving for bananas like she does. In other words see it from inside her skin."

"You sound like my mother."

"Now nobody ever told me that before!" He grins at me. "When you *understand* that girl then you have to forget the whole thing and give it to your hands. Your eyes lie all the time; but your hands don't lie. Quit trying to picture it before your hands can show it to you."

Pictures slide behind my eyes.

"You are trying to make a copy of Raccoon in Capital Letters. The Essence of Coon or some bit like that. I hate animals, but you're supposed to care about this particular mother."

I relax a little at his use of this familiar word.

"Think of it," he continues, "like a bowl: if any part is wrong, the whole thing leaks. Don't keep looking at it to see if the head's *right* or the feet are *right*, whatever that means. You got to remember your eyes lie."

"I don't trust my hands yet. My three-year-old—"

"Right! It's all downhill after three." He stops a minute and looks around. Then he digs in a pocket for a cigarette. "I have another longer talk I give my culturettes, but let's have a cigarette and you can start again."

"No, thanks, I don't—"

"Judas, I never trust nonsmokers. Oral types are the only kind. Here, chew on some of this wax, then."

That's what smells like oil fields. He has given me a piece of brown tarlike wax, piles of which have dried on every table.

"That's the stuff," he explains, "we build up to melt out to make these beautiful bronze mothers. Are you with me?"

He leads me to a shelf with three bronze figures. They are all women, and I don't see at first that they are all pregnant because they are so different. One is a large woman, really just a torso leaning back on thick arms, chin sunk on her chest; one is leaning heavy elbows on foreshortened knees, making a sort of round cage around a thick belly; one is a standing slip of girl with her hands clutching her wide stomach: she has little stubby legs and it is—*me*.

Tears crowd out of my eyes and I lick them off my cheeks.

"What's that for?" he wants to know.

Pointing I explain, "That's *me*."

"Egomania! All of you have Egomania." He blows smoke while I wipe my face. "Clara Blue, let's go make a raccoon." He laughs.

For an hour or more he wanders around smoking

and peering over my shoulder, or standing at my elbow, his head coming no taller than mine, his rasping breath at my ear undoing my calm.

For an hour or more a hungry mammal with wide curving back picks at crackers in a box. She is two years old, very hungry, at the feeding tray for the first time. Babies are at home. She has followed a large, smugger raccoon to my yard, but she is still jumpy. Her coat is spotty, rubbed thin in places: there are fleas or something around the tail. Her eyes are not trusting; she does not know that in zoos you can get your supper just by washing copper pennies for the children who file by.

For more than an hour my hands are drier than I like, my face sweatier.

"Okay," he says at last.

"It's hard with you watching—"

"You'll forget I'm here after a while."

But I don't think I will, ever.

"Wander over here." He guides me and we look at some of his classes' ash trays and madonnas and vases: nothing to make tears on this trip around. Then he leads me back to my clay.

"Look at it."

I do and I see that it isn't good.

"See? Clumsy and half scared to death—you not her —but still, it's a place to begin. You want to come back?"

"I can come on Tuesdays and Thursdays from nine until twelve. My three-year-old—"

He throws up his hands. "You've got to be kidding. Somehow I get the message that you were born in the middle of last week! I charge five dollars a body a half hour in my ash-tray classes. At the rate you're trying to move in that would cost you about one twenty a month. Maybe I should offer to sell you a part interest in the leaky plumbing."

"But I want—"

"I know." He looks at the ceiling. "Well, look, come on and hide over there somewhere in the unfinished work I don't want to look at. Maybe I won't remember you're here. Maybe I'll manage to give you an hour's worth of attention once a week from the great master; maybe a few choice and inspiring words worth about five dollars a week wholesale."

"Locke! You don't need to do that. I didn't think—"

"If you're going to remember my name it'll cost you more. Just something simple like Master or Teacher will do." He grins at me and grabs my hand in what must mean it's a bargain and I can go.

Reluctantly I make myself go. Not before looking for a time at the bronze girl clutching her stomach; not before seeing that Locke is deep in scraping one of the shiny figures with acid, and has forgotten that I exist. With envy for his condition I close the door behind me.

CHAPTER

{ 5 }

I HAVE my back to the fire watching a few snowflakes melt against the library window and waiting for our old friends to come for supper: Sarah, who was my roommate at school, and her husband, Hayes, who teaches with Anslow. The library, which catches the north wind, is Anslow's room. It has all his books and notes that he is working on and a faint smell of leather.

I stand and catch my breath, enjoying the warmth on the back of my legs. The disorder of socks and newspapers and kitchen pans is out of sight; there are fresh mushrooms in the stew; and the boys are tucked down for the night.

As I left my sons with their bedtime books I was reminded again how much they grow each year, yet how each evening they seem exactly the same as they did the night before. Although I never see them change, it is necessary to know that each night's few words and story add the imperceptible silt that at the end of the year makes another layer.

The table is set in blues and whites like the winter world outside. I like to have it seem cold to the eye inside when it is cold outside: it is an effort to reinforce Texas's brief seasons.

When it is hot outside I like to see hot oranges and yellows inside echoing the burning sun. Between the heat and cold are brief weeks of fall and spring, weeks which bring rain in the good years and bouquets of leaves and flowers into the house.

Anslow has a drink ready when they come and after supper we come back again to the fire with our brandy. The men have talked about the news in the paper and schedules in their classrooms, but men who do the same thing get into a problem talking because what they have in common they don't do the same way.

They come to sit with us when they have run out of words.

Sturdy brown-haired Sarah tucks her feet up under her pink shirtwaist and asks Anslow about his book. She works on many projects, moving from public kindergartens to mental retardation as she feels the needs of the community call for it. She tells him about her latest job, which is tutoring dropouts, and ties this into one of the themes of Anslow's book.

As Hayes shifts his great bulk down into an easy

chair like a dog by the hearth, we talk about his boys and his general. His three sons, two of whom are the ages of ours, are named for Civil War generals—Lee, Jeb, and baby Jackson.

He says after a long story about his boys and their Sunday-school teacher, "You know, Clara, you and I are the only white Baptists left in the South. All the rest have got educated and divided themselves into Episcopalians and Unitarians. In my spare time, whenever that is, I'm going to figure out which of those groups is *in* and which is *out*."

I smile at him. "We Baptists are becoming extinct."

"We need a preservation society."

I ask him for my favorite story. "Tell me about Marthanne."

"She still waits on the bridge, honey, for the general's aide."

"And the general is still in the tent?"

"He is! He's still poring over those battle plans while daylight and the enemy crawl up the ravine." He shakes with pleasure thinking of his people, shakes his chins like a great bulldog.

He loves them so. Anslow swears that Hayes will never finish his book. He may be right, for to me Hayes's characters wait forever like figures on a Greek vase. Some evenings, after a few more drinks, Hayes will stand me in a corner and tell me the whole story: that there is a time in each man's life when part of him goes out to a woman for the first time. Here he puts his thick hand on his chest. His eyes are seeing Marthanne and the aide on the covered bridge. Then he will tell about how each man comes to a point in his life when a decision has to be made. He gazes at the general, who comes out of the tent to lead his men to utter defeat. As he tells it, I see them, too.

But Sarah chases away our friends now by reminding us, "Hayes has put red pins on his wall map by way of promising me that he *is* working on his book."

But Hayes winks at me as he says, "You are herewith invited to come down and see my red pins for yourself." His look says that *we* know those people aren't going to go anywhere. To Anslow he says good night as he pulls himself up out of the chair with some effort. "Anslow, we got to get on. Now that you're published maybe you can sit up all night, but the masses need to get up before the sun. Besides, your wife's dinner has put me to sleep."

He gives me a good-night hug.

That was pleasant and I am sleepy too. But as I start back to bed Anslow says in a hurt voice, "You even remember the *name* of the girl on Hayes's bridge!"

It is not something I can explain, the difference between his book and Hayes's book. We go to bed without talking.

When he is asleep I go down into the woods to see the differences between the two raccoons, and am rewarded by the blinking musty presence of my surviving friend the possum.

CHAPTER

"WATER is everything!" I whisper to Clyde.

But all he knows is that when it rains we don't get up. He lies curled up between my knees as I watch the rainstorm soak our dry escarpment. We are only a rain away from a plain, a water table away from a desert.

Gusty winds bring the smell of water and the grapey smell of blooming mountain laurel in through the open window. It is very sweet.

"Water is everything!" I tell Anslow as he comes out of his morning shower. He is damp, too.

"You're still in bed." He looks pleased.

"Raining—"

He sits on the side of the bed. "It's good to see you like this."

He is wrapped in a towel and his face is not yet pulled together for the day. His balding head has water on the blond strands; his unshaved face is loose and stubbled. I like that.

Reaching for his hand, I ask, "Did you get the quizzes graded?"

He is happy that I remembered. "Most of them. The lack of literacy is staggering this year: they pile a series of paragraphs that make absolutely no sense one on top of the other and hand it in believing they've done a paper."

"You have some good students."

"Fewer this year." A moment of doubt makes furrows around his eyes. "Do I say that every year?"

"An—Texas is becoming a desert. . . ." I confide my worry to him as he has done to me about the classes.

But this makes him get up. "Let's don't go through that one again."

I have reminded him of a bad fight, I guess. He remembers fights as distinct bad times; to me what we have are reoccurrences of the same impasse that exists in how we see the world. What he calls fights go something like this:

He will raise his voice, "It is a mystery to me how you can get so worked up about things like that water table and where Andromeda has drifted to today, yet not get even slightly involved in the coming election. When was the last time you read a newspaper?"

This causes me to draw in my breath and retort, "When Garfield was shot."

"All right, be funny, but I am trying to say that you are talking about changes that will take centuries and over which we have absolutely no control, whereas I am talking about decisions we must make *now:* changes we must effect for this country if our children are to survive. You are the one that always talks about *survival.*"

But then I get mad and say something like, "Don't fall off that technological precipice again. I just meant that galaxies are moving away from each other, and animals are mutating, and Texas is becoming a desert, all right under your nose, and you can't see it unless someone reports it to you in print."

"You make it sound like a criminal offense to keep up with what is going on in the world."

But he does not understand that what I tell him is true. These things are happening whether we see them or not. As Mother would put it: *The star burns, the red bird calls without your eyes and ears.*

Not wanting to go through that now, Anslow forces a smile. "I'll see if the paper is here. Bet it's soaked. That paperboy never wraps it when it rains." He turns at the door. "Shall I bring some coffee?"

"I can get up—"

"Stay there."

A flood crashes against the pecan tree, shaking a wave of branches against the window. A gray mocker scissors onto a limb, shakes water from her coat, complains loudly. Deep in the woods mouths and roots are reaching for water. It comes so seldom; it runs off so fast.

As we have our coffee, the deep grape smell hangs in the rainy air.

Anslow says as he puts on his tie, "Don't forget that we are going to a movie with Evan and Louise."

"You told me. Are we going to eat first?"

"I thought we might. I have the rest of these papers to do, but I will plan to get through." He combs his hair. "I got the boys up, but you'd better see about them."

"True. They hate late breakfast." I sit up in my gown. "Do you have a class with Mr. Smith today?"

"Yes."

"How are the lessons going?"

"I don't know. I can't tell if I am getting any better. Did I tell you that he has a bronze figure of a girl with stubby legs grabbing her middle with big hands and she looks just like me?" I slip out of my gown and demonstrate for him, standing just like the bronze girl.

"God, the way you see yourself."

But this *is* me. I ask him, "How do *you* see me?"

He laughs. "Undressed." But then he sighs and says seriously, "With more charity than you give me credit for, Clara."

CHAPTER

{ 7 }

I LET myself in the carriage-house door, rain at my back. Awkwardly I work for an hour until Locke notices, or until he can pull himself out of the waxy pregnancy he is building all over a table in the corner near the burners.

"Good morning, Clara Blue."

"It's still the same."

"Stand away and let me have a look."

He doesn't say anything.

I tell him, "Her head isn't right." The elongated face of the possum hangs heavy above the picky fingers.

He shrugs.

"Maybe if I set it farther back, here—?"

He looks all around the room; looks at his bony fingernails.

"Locke, help me!"

"It's a vessel, I told you. If it's got a hole in it it leaks out. It can't be good except for the head: if the head is wrong the opossum doesn't exist."

"Oh, Locke."

"Don't begin the sad bit. Like my culturette classes: they want to be Brancusi and Lipchitz, tomorrow, tomorrow by nine fifteen."

"I've worked four—well, almost four weeks on her."

"The big crucifixion! The trouble is, like I told you about that raccoon we made until she died, that you don't know this particular girl."

"Maybe if the ears—"

"Like this?" He grabs a mass of clay and mocks up great floppy cocker-spaniel ears. Even as a joke they look better than mine. It's like Cal hammering out better shapes on the kitchen table . . .

"What do you know about her? Does she have fleas? Can she scratch if she does? Does she smell? Did she take a leak in the water pan? Is she leching after her neighbor's old man?"

"But—"

"Where does she sleep? What particular tree? How high on the branches? Judas, I hate animals, but *you're* supposed to know all this bit."

"All right."

"You've got to trust your hands."

"You've forgotten because it comes so easy for you."

"Easy? Me? I crawl across this floor at two a.m. and

come back red-eyed the following dawn. I don't eat; I don't sleep; I'm in a trance, having a vision, a fix, a great thing. Blood sweats out my armpits. I make the best thing I ever made: better. The best thing the world has ever seen: better. Strong men will weep when it is unveiled; virgins will offer themselves. That clay monger from Dallas will take up basketweaving. Ah! Then it is finished. I step back to admire: and it's a dozen others made from a mold on sale at Woolworth's."

I laugh at him. "Okay, all right, you don't need to go through that whole act for me."

"You don't like my style?" He pretends to be offended.

"I do." Which is true.

"It's a defense. You know. What everybody needs. You need one."

"They're hard to get through."

"That's the point of a defense, right?"

"Like a shell."

"Judas, before you begin the anthropomorphic bit why don't you shut up and get to work and let me get to work."

"Her ears aren't right."

"Work until your eyes get so tired they blunk out like Little Orphan Annie's and your hands can take over. Look at that opossum: it's lousy. How's that for teaching method?"

"Drop dead."

"That's what I want to hear."

He disappears toward his pot of wax.

My hands return to smash the lousy trial-run mammal. I love possums, but this must be one special possum.

I picture the dark spiky one with its stiff bare tail that I watched eating spaghetti and part of a paper plate after the raccoons had gone. She is the ugliest and the darkest one who has come. Her face peering out from the mangy coat was a tattletale gray. Looking at the gray rain sliding down the windows high above I try to see a gray face.

To the sound of the downpour my hands grope for that face and I work for the rest of the morning. Work until the smell of oil fields gradually gives way to the smell of mountain laurel in my mind.

"Go home," Locke says at my elbow. "The three-year-old and all that."

"Look at it."

"You want a pat on the back."

He is unkind.

"For reduced rates you only get one pat a month."

I look at it myself: it is rough. The outline is too blurred to tell about her, but she exists. It isn't a copy, but it is hesitant, uncertain. Through a sheet of rain there is the suggestion of a face. It is—as Locke would put it—a place to begin.

"Okay, Locke, see you Thursday."

"Leaving without the Master's verdict?"

"Who needs it?"

"Clara!"

"I said who needs it?"

He grins at me. "Sometimes I think you were born in the middle of last week."

For the first time he does not grab my hand goodbye, and I think that it means something. One of these days I am going to see *him* not so blurred and then it will be even harder to go out the door of the carriage house.

CHAPTER

{ 8 }

THE night air is clear and fresh, blowing cold at the edges, as we walk with Evan and Louise down a wet street by the campus after the movie. Cars coming from behind us make splashing sounds, their head-lights spilling out pools of rainbows as they pass. In the silence between cars we can hear a few whippoorwills call out from the rainy darkness.

The walk is quiet on the way to a crowded snack shop where we stop. Anslow hummed tonight as he was get-ting dressed and took his time deciding over a tie. Now getting us all seated for late coffee and pie he smooths down the strands of his hair and hums again.

The last time we saw Evan and Louise was at the dinner at our house to celebrate An's book. That night Evan seemed the sort of man who when you smile at him to show you are being friendly doesn't smile back and then after you become uncomfortable he laughs. He is short and dark with a sharp nose and soft hands.

At our dinner he told Anslow that he, Evan, had done legal articles on the same theory as Anslow's book: articles that quoted one source and then another source and finally, after concluding that there was no unassailable conclusion, became an article that someone else could quote.

Anslow enjoyed that, agreeing, which wasn't true, that his book was a warm hash of secondary source material on its way to becoming another secondary source.

Louise, a pale girl with nervous hands, chided the men. "You both get such a pleasure out of selling yourselves short. You're too confident it's a joke. Let me tell you that you may end up like my poor old Daddy who, tongue in cheek, made a production of assuming an aura of failure in the midst of success. The only trouble was, that being a literal and dutiful daughter, I took him at his word and considered him pretty much nobody until years after he died."

Anslow called her an ungrateful child, which made her smile and brought color to her white cheeks.

Now she is flushed like that while they talk about the movie.

It was an Italian film about people looking for each other, told through such wonderful camerawork that the subtitles did not distract. At times the lens narrowed the eyes, blurring the nearby faces and focusing on a distant face, as your own eyes do searching for someone across the room at a party. Then, melting away that scene as if washing it with rain, the lens widened and moved in closer and closer until the face grew as a face does when it comes nearer and nearer to your own, first making every hair and pore seem clear and large, then coming too close to focus on as it touches yours. It was beautiful photography.

Louise says, "I did like it, every minute of it. Why are you men nervous about stories where the hero wanders anywhere he has a mind to? Watching him climb out of his sports car in the Roman night scares you." She leans across to Anslow. "Admit that you were keeping your historical distance. Admit that you were watching *The Decline and Fall of Rome!*"

Anslow laughs. "Even if I *had* tried to keep my distance it would have been impossible with you jumping around in the seat next to me."

She laughs at that.

Evan says in a voice that makes fun of them, "Louise wiggles around at all these modern searches for meaning. Hate to disappoint you, Blue, but it wasn't because you were in the next seat: she's trying out for the lead role. When I flew her to New York for a play about a bunch of unhappy people we had a little trouble with her: she kept crawling over the footlights."

Louise explains to me with exaggerated slowness, "Evan doesn't mean that *he* flew the plane to New York; he doesn't mean he *piloted* the plane when he says he flew me to New York. He means that it cost money and he wants you to know that he paid the money."

Evan leans back in his chair and taps me with a soft finger. "Louise is emphasizing to you folks that I care only for the material things of life and do not appreciate the finer side of culture. In case, you know, that she should ever need witnesses." He leans toward us and lowers his voice. "Talking of money, which we always do, reminds me of my first case. It was only a ten-dollar job and as I showed my boss the green bill he said to me, 'Now that's wonderful, boy, that's good experience for you when you get ready to handle your *smaller* cases!' "

As they laugh Louise says, "Evan, you made that up on the spot."

He peers at her down his nose. "Now whatever made you think that?"

"For one thing, you never had a boss."

I am relieved if it is all a joke. In the pause I wonder if their children always know how to take what they say, and, foolishly, as it has nothing to do with the conversation, I ask, "You have two daughters?"

Evan answers, "We sure do. We have two daughters. Two young things named Daphne and Diana. Louise uses up all her time on them, worrying that they'll be chased but still chaste." He spells the words for us to be sure we have it. "And worrying to be sure they'll marry better than she did."

She makes a face at him. "They look like Snow White and Rose Red. Do you remember that story? Daphne is as dark as Evan, and Diana is blonder than I am." She stares at her white hands, then says, "I can't leave them alone. I nag at them too much. Nag at them to wash their hair, or pick up their clothes, or hold their heads up and *smile*." She looks at Anslow. "I bet you don't go through all that with boys, do you?"

He answers her seriously. "You wonder about what they'll do. To make a living. About their education."

We have never talked about that. In vain I try to picture Cal and Arch as grown boys, as men, but I only see them change into my father and Anslow.

Evan pounces on my hesitation. "You don't worry about that, do you, Clara? You just want to get them big enough where they're not killing themselves or someone else, maybe?"

I tell him lightly, "I just take it one day at a time."

"Well," he says, "Either your husband keeps them under perfect control, or you're keeping your head in the sand."

I show him. "Buried up to here."

"You mean Blue has lost his control?"

They all laugh, and Louise tells me, "Evan loves to set traps."

In the car after we let them out I move closer to Anslow for the drive home.

"You have a good time?" he asks.

"I liked the movie." But this is evasive, so I say, "Sometimes I don't know how to take what they say. Their fighting can sound so real."

He pats my leg. "They just kid around. They both enjoy it; it's a habit, back and forth like that. It's good they can do that and not have to worry all the time about hurting each other's feelings."

"You enjoyed it."

"Sure. It was relaxing." He was silent awhile and then asks, "You doing all right?"

"Sure."

His voice is anxious—it lets me realize fully that he has to worry about how I am doing.

As we turn down our street I ask, "Do you really think about what Arch and Cal will do when they are grown?"

He says, "From time to time. It's natural to wonder."

And I wonder, as we pull up the driveway, what I would say to that if I kidded around.

Much later by the feeder trays I sit on the damp ground and smell the rain in the air. I hear many more shapes moving through the wet underbrush than my eyes can see.

CHAPTER

{ 9 }

THE hills are leafed a pale green. Daylight now comes at 5:45 a.m. and the birds and I are full of the new piece of time we have. Over steaming coffee we smell the sweet honeysuckle, which makes us chatter loudly.

All over the grass birds are eating. Two large roadrunners have walked up through the woods to where we are sitting. One is ruffing the front of his chest; the other has a grasshopper in her mouth. Fat Clyde is stiff: here are intruders who should be chased—but the size? The mocker shouts at them, the jay shrieks and dives, until—unhurried—the giant wild birds stroll back through the sumac out of sight.

I think about the clay waiting with Locke, and about the fresh April daylight (as Mother would put it:

Today you have today) until Clyde reminds me by bounding in my lap that it is time to eat.

Over eggs Arch has no great smile.

"What is it, Arch?"

"Nothing."

"*What?*"

"I said nothing." His small chin-jutting voice sounds like me saying "Who needs it," and I have to laugh.

My laughter sends him flying from the room.

"What is it, Arch?" I locate him.

"Do I have to tell you?"

"No."

"Well, it's Show-and-Tell, that's all. And I don't have anything that anybody will listen to. All this stuff—" He looks glumly around his room.

"Did you take this map?"

"In *first* grade!"

"Let's go look outside."

There isn't much: a feather from one of the road-runners. We look down in the tunnel where the four armadillo babies must be hiding, but of course they are not to be seen. He rejects all offers of apple or pear blooms. By this time An is sticking his head out saying, "Come on, Archer, we'll be late."

So the roadrunner feather is it.

"Arch—?"

"Thanks."

"Are you okay?"

"Sure!" And he is gone.

There are legions of things about boys who are eight that I do not understand, but his lack of defenses I do understand. Arch is so vulnerable in the in-between age: neither little like Cal, for whom everything is black and white, nor safe and grown like his father, for whom everything is again black and white. He is in that gray world where you can care a lot about a lot of things: where things can still hurt. When I was eight I carried everything that hurt me off to the creek to look at it alone.

It would be nice if I could put a coat around him against the world, but you can't do for someone else what you cannot do for yourself.

Promising Cal that I have not forgotten that it is my day to pick up Lee for school, I stop An to remind him that we are going to Sarah and Hayes's for supper.

He groans. "I was going to get to those outlines tonight."

"It's just us going."

"I know we have to go. But Hayes is being touchy about school: we can't talk about anything except average rainfalls or grass fires."

"We can look at the new pins on his map."

"So we can." He looks at his watch and heads to the car.

"Mama," Cal says. "We need to go."

But we have time to straighten the house a little and find his other shoe.

In the car we go through our ritual.

"How are you and Miss May?"

"She makes me sit on a chair if I don't pick up every-thing."

"And Mark and David?"

"We got some boards that they don't to frame our sidewalk."

"And Lisa, and Debbie and Patty?"

"Those girls play in the kitchen corner all morning."

"And Normally?" Normally is what he calls the new girl with red hair.

"She just sometimes comes and helps us. She just sometimes puts little pieces of gravel in the wet sand to make it concrete."

"After all the rain I can see that you need concrete. Let's go get Lee."

"His baby Jackson bit him yesterday."

What a nice thought for a green, blooming honey-suckle of a morning. "Great!" I tell my son.

CHAPTER

I LET myself in the door of the room where I live. Everything that doesn't matter is forgotten as soon as I am inside.

Locke is not here. There is a quick minute of disappointment before my hands unwrap the clay. My mind is on Arch and the feather. I can still see his eight-year-old chin-jutting face this morning. Unnoticed, my hands begin to work.

Without direction, because my mind is caring very much about that boy, they move and build a shape. Casually they warm up. Casually, as if I were stroking the cat in the sunshine, they move back and forth curving around the softness of a shape. It is some time before my eyes notice that it is an armadillo baby, a light-scared child in a suit of paper armor against the world.

I know all about him: he sleeps with his back to the dry dirt, nestled against his three identical brothers. But my mind wanders to Arch as my hands work very slowly.

With care they make the creases on the bony back, but faintly because he is so young; with care they put his shut tight eyes and sloping nose together into a small face.

"So." Locke stands coughing at my elbow, looking at what I'm working on.

"So who needs it." I laugh because this is now a joke.

He grins at me. "Time for a cigarette."

We sit and he smokes.

After a minute he looks off and says, "Clara Blue, we have to decide what to do with you. This problem hasn't come up before with my ash-tray ladies, but even with that first dumb coon there was no doubt that you had this little talent."

"Do you charge extra for these speeches?"

"Exorbitantly. What to do today is to decide what you want to do with it. You can't spend your life making a zoo to pass the time while the three-year-old is away."

"You said I could do some wax things."

"Judas, you can do a stable of bronzes if you want.

That costs money, of course, melting out the wax and casting. I'm not talking about that; I'm talking about do you want to sell them on the open market? Put your bodies out on the street? Enter them in shows? Show the world the Essence of Coon and all that."

"I never thought about that."

"That's the thing about you, Clara Blue."

With caution I looked at his light eyes. They are almost closed, wrinkled at the corners, watching me. Something claws at my stomach but I keep looking at his eyes. "Locke, what did you do before you did this all the time?"

"Drank."

"For a living."

"It seems to me, now that you ask, that I taught somewhere. It's a haze."

"How did you happen to—to do this?"

"It's easier on the liver. I used to drink until the ground came up to meet the sky. It makes a great sound when they hit together like that, bang. The next morning I'd check my clothes and if there was grass stain on my front I'd know there hadn't been anybody under me when I slept. But after a while waiting for the noise they made crashing together, I forgot the bottle. It was pretty simple, really. So I got this place. No more grass stains."

"I understand."

"Deliver me from being understood!"

"I just mean I know about that sound."

He smokes awhile.

I say, "Locke, when I looked up your name in the phone book I was afraid that it wasn't your real name: that your real name was Claude Abbott, Abbott with two *t*s."

"It is, of course." There is a pause. "What did you do?"

"Before this?"

"Before you knocked at my door."

"When the boys were little I took them to Travis Park when things got bad, and swung on the big metal swings while they played around. I still go there sometimes just to swing. When things get where I can't handle them."

"That's the big park with the creek behind it?"

"Over behind the post office."

"Now I know where to look for you."

"Now you know."

There is a silence I can feel before he speaks again. "Okay, Clara Blue, shall we put that defenseless animal up for sale?"

"Sure." I give him Arch's smile as best I can remember it.

"Sometimes I think . . ." He touches my arm lightly as we go to look at the pots of wax and he begins to tell me how to build up wax figures for casting.

CHAPTER

{ 11 }

BLINDED by light eyes I stop my car at Travis Park on the way home. Under large live oaks the dusty ground slopes down to a dry creek bed. Through the leaves the sunlight filters: I know eyes brighter than today's hesitant sun.

I swing on the great metal swings where high-school boys linger to push high-school girls in the late afternoons, behind the vacant field where they throw footballs, in front of the small chair-swings with bars for toddlers to hold. No one else is in the park.

Deliver Locke, as he would put it, from being understood by me. But he does speak to my condition. When he talks of a place to begin, it is my mother saying: *You have only to know that wherever you are you are on*

the road to yourself. When he talks about the sky and
earth smashing together it is what happens for me in
our part of the woods as the sun first turns on our faces
in the mornings.

One other time there was a man I could not get out
of my mind: very tall and fair. While I had my hands
in formaldehyde comparing backbones, he had his feet
rooted in the lessons of the past and his eyes fixed on
the promise of the future.

I guess that's still the way we are, but it seems different. Now he keeps tripping over me down here on my
hands and knees in the present.

Pushing my swing with dusty shoes high in the
empty air, I go back to that nice time ten years ago.

A small girl that was me sat wrapped in a huge coat
down to her ankles on the edge of a lily-pad pond waiting for a tall boy. Black goldfish swam beneath the
dark water, shadows meeting the long shadows cast by
the overhanging roof of the zoology building, under
the winter sun. Short legs were pulled under my coat,
wide hands lay restless in my pockets.

I was in the middle of a crisis between getting into
and getting out of school. I had trouble accepting the
difference between a bird laid out on the lab table as
an example of bone structure and a bird as he dived
under the trees.

Cutting up animals, I was losing rather than gaining
knowledge about them. With every vertebrate and in-
vertebrate fact I knew less and less about living. I

wanted to see the anatomical differences as a function of a struggling, surviving species, to translate warm-blooded and cold-blooded from words into shapes.

I bought some clay from the store that supplied the art students and worked out models of all the animals we were comparing: rough damp outlines that started almost as skeletons and grew into suggestions of living mammals, birds, and reptiles. It did not answer all I wanted to know about what being alive meant, but it was a start.

That is the year I met Anslow, through Sarah's boyfriend Hayes. At the time I was giving kisses in the afternoons on a blanket out by the river to a rancher's son. He was warm-blooded and had some backbone. He was one of the few boys I liked who didn't spend most of his time hanging around our house waiting in vain for my father to sound like a great scholar.

There was a little time when Anslow and I would talk on our porch until past midnight almost every night, and the rancher's son and I would watch fall come to the trees along the bluffs in the afternoons and talk about cattle.

But by the time I waited for Anslow by the pond in late February there was no one but him.

Catching sight of him coming across the campus I would fling myself at his chest, amazed that such a fine, tall man, who knew where the world had been and where it was headed, could care for me.

Daddy explained marriage at that time with a theory

of selectivity based on individual anatomy. In other words, people married each other because they looked like someone in their past who had mattered to them. For instance, he had a grandmother who rocked all day, her short feet barely reaching the ground, snapping beans and gazing at the world with a serene freckled face.

He decided Anslow looked like my Grandfather Callison, whom I loved very much. Grandfather used to let me get up at dawn with him to feed the birds on his back porch, looking out across the levee, the summers I visited him in Tennessee.

He had a narrow balding head, trim blond mustache, and gentle hands.

When Anslow and I were engaged and going to Libertyville in East Texas to see his family I looked for someone he had cared for that might look like me.

We had driven, sitting close and very much in love, across the state through rolling sandy hills timbered with loblolly pines, peopled with dairy farmers tending cows in lush meadows, prospering from the yield of chugging oil pumps called grasshoppers, to a town where all the streets were named for trees.

It was a good visit. Anslow's mother had overcome a blinding migraine to welcome me with a small coffee to meet her garden club. I could have been back in Grandmother Callison's house, except there was coffee instead of tea, pecan buns instead of black walnut bread. While

the ladies looked me over we talked of Anslow and his
much older brother, a New Orleans gynecologist who
had a beautiful wife. They admired my ring and told
about their gardens and asked about my family.

Mary Blue presided graciously in a way that was,
like my grandmother, rather corseted and effusive.

My mother used to tell of helping her own mother in
Alabama serve butter cakes and sherry at a dessert
party for one of her sewing club who had had some of
her favorite poems published for the club's enjoyment.
Mother stood in a yellow silk dress behind her mother's
chair watching the ladies admire the verse. I felt much
like that girl in yellow with the ladies of Libertyville,
and therefore I felt very much at home.

After supper, Archy—Anslow's father—told us stories in the back yard under the pecan trees. Leaning
back in his chair and assuming an East Texas drawl, he
gave us the juicy bits of his general practice. Whenever
he got to a line like "That ninety-year-old isn't going to
meet his Maker as long as he can still get his house-
keeper under the bedsheets," Anslow's mother would
remember that we needed to finish tidying up inside.

Helping her fix up the living room I found a framed
picture of the woman I had hoped to see: a plain woman,
low to the ground, with strong arms that used to hold
Anslow close when his mother had a headache. It was
his Grandmother Blue, who stayed with them for ten
years.

Thinking of her on the long drive with Anslow back to school, I was content in my mind that he wanted the girl he had.

The smell of pine was with us in the dark, and the smell of crude oil. Grasshoppers pumped along the road between patches of Guernsey. The state's few remaining gas flares looked like fireflies in the dark. Anslow built castles in the air for us, floated promises on the moat of our future.

But in the present it is time to let the swing rock to a stop, to go get Cal, and to leave my thoughts of Locke with him, bending over his work in the carriage house.

CHAPTER

{ 12 }

THE night is so pleasant we have walked hand in hand down our long street that smells of honeysuckle to Sarah and Hayes's house.

I like to go to their house because it is always the same, and that is a comfort. Hayes is at the door when we come, making welcoming noises and taking up a lot of space. It is good to watch this heavy man claim his territory in a room like a bear in a forest.

Over drinks the men begin to talk about grass fires. It seems that fires can start in dry grass if the sun's rays come through a broken Coke bottle at just the right angle.

Sarah has her shoes off and is talking about her boys. "Did Cal tell you about Normally?"

"That's the girl with red hair."

"I told Hayes I thought my mental-retardation work had gone to my head when Lee came home from nursery school talking about Normally. You know that Lee—he always tells such wild stories anyway."

Sarah's boys are totally predictable to her. She says with certainty that "Lee always—," or "Jeb is just never—," or "Baby Jackson is certain to—." It gives me a feeling of security that I don't get with my own sons.

She is explaining, "But it turned out that Normally is a vision of four-year-old loveliness—I saw her yesterday myself, with waist-length hair, and you're right, it *is* red, really red—whose real name is *Norma Lee!*"

After we talk about school awhile I say, "This weather reminds me of springs when I was little and the creeks were full. We played Ophelia drowning and looked for crawdads."

"That's what you were doing in school, looking at crawdads, as you call them."

I know the bottled crustaceans she is remembering. It gives me a picture of our crowded dormitory room. "They took up less space than your drawing boards and campaign posters."

She looks younger as she thinks back to that time. "I *was* always running for something, wasn't I? That didn't mix too well with art school." She smiles. "But look who turned into the artist."

"Not me. Mr. Smith makes me compare backbones again, so I'm right at home." Which is true.

After supper we visit a little with the men, who are tired of relocating pins on the map, in the familiar pink-and-brown-flowered living room where first Jeb and Arch, and then Cal and Lee, and now Baby Jackson have unloaded the brass magazine stand and chewed on the copper kettle that holds logs and pulled ivy out of a holder Sarah calls a jardiniere. A large sleeping boxer lies near us on his favorite spot on the rug, which he has worn smooth.

I ask Hayes, "How is Marthanne?"

"On the bridge." He puts his hand on his chest.

"And the general?"

"In that tent. He's thinking, though, don't worry, he *is* thinking." He loosens his tie and asks me, "You still working twice a week on your clay business?"

"Still working, don't worry."

He leans back in the chair. "I was thinking about that the other day, about how you used to carry on about those cave paintings. Guess you finally decided to decorate your own cave."

"I don't do anything as good as those, the ones out West or at Lascaux. But I'm working."

"Well, I remember that you had it figured that the women drew while the men hunted, so I thought we better tell Anslow he should get himself a mastodon trap, or at least a raccoon trap." He loves his idea and laughs until his chins shake.

Anslow doesn't enjoy it, so I tell them something else about the clay. "I do have some news about what I'm working on now: my teacher is going to enter some of my things is a show."

Sarah claps her hands. "Why didn't you tell me?"

Anslow looks hurt and tells her, "Don't feel bad, Sarah, this is the first I've heard of it, too."

When we get home he is still unhappy.

"You didn't mention it at all. We walked all the way to their house and you didn't mention a word about it."

"I forgot."

"You couldn't have." He sits on the bed and begins to take off his shoes.

"I did." I take off my dress. "I wasn't thinking about this morning, I was thinking about going to their house to eat. But now that we are, I did do something nice this morning. . . . I stopped at the park where we used to sit at night, Travis Park, and swung and thought about the first time we drove to Libertyville, and the times you met me at the zoology pond. Anslow, those were good times."

"Did you?" He takes off his shirt. "I remember that park all right. *And* the pond. You were cute sitting out there, sweetheart, in the freezing cold." He reaches out for me. "You jumped up when you saw me and ran down that path whether there were a dozen people in the way or not. You had a notebook that the pages kept falling out of when you ran."

"I was glad to see you."

"Are you now?" He asks with his mouth by my ear.

"Yes."

"We shouldn't fight."

He keeps me close as he turns out the light.

Making love, I feel that Anslow is glad that it is *me* in his arms and I am content.

I sleep, content, until the raccoons wake me by shaking the limbs of the pecan tree against my window.

CHAPTER

{ 13 }

YESTERDAY Mother wrote (on a scrap of paper attached to a clipping about Daddy) part of a poem she likes, something I think of Edith Sitwell's:

Each clustered bouquet of the snow is
Like stephanotis and white roses.

I know what she was thinking of: her world has melted the snow and mine is steeped in white flowers. She must be picturing the deep black bowls we fill each May with all the white yard flowers: climbing roses, cape jasmine, snapdragons, bitter oleander blooms. It is the only time flowers come into the house.

This morning when I came out at 5:30 a.m. the birds had been up for hours walking around on the grass eating. Sprinklers all down the street had made the air damp. Clyde coughed up a fur ball he swallowed because his coat is shedding to get ready for the heat. It is no longer possible to get up early enough to catch it cool; no longer possible to make the coffee hot enough to make a contrast between the inside and the outside of my stomach.

Thinking of Mother, I filled the bowls with round profusions of blossoms; thinking that May is a restless time between the sweetness of April and the motionless baking stretches of summer.

Other years in May I have been full of the end of school, mine or the boys', or Anslow's. He always wishes he were leaving his classes with more, wishes he had "more to show," as he would put it.

This May I have waked in the nights with Locke's name before me. Waked to lie in bed feeling very much like a girl.

But I am learning: each animal I work has a face now, each one in her picture frame is separate and different and matters to me. Locke has been a good teacher, and I hang on to that thought as I let myself in the door of my home, the carriage house, and focus on the wax.

He is not here, which helps. Kicking off my shoes I soften the brush, wiping it back and forth on the shelf until it loosens. To get the smell inside my head I chew a piece of petroleum tar.

How I hate to begin. Stalling, I wander around look-

ing at Locke's current piece. It is a great welded man;
it has wings from the shoulders, wings which may melt
when he flies too near the sun (but I don't like to get
into that sort of allegory and of course Locke does not
think about it like that). Anyway, it is about four feet
high, very gaunt from the front. Thin planes form his
chest and connect at a slight angle to other planes
which form his legs. At complete right angles are the
peaked coat-hanger-type spires of his wings. It is very
good, of course.

Stalling, I test the wax heating in the pan on the
hotplate. I stir it around and it breaks up into icebergs.
I set the pan back, then test it again, and again, until it
is melted but thick. I unwrap the brown mummy from
her Saran Wrap. (I can't leave my pieces lying around
carelessly on the shelves like so many corpses. I'm not
as sure as Locke is that there are plenty more coming
from where this one came from.)

No longer able to escape, I dip the brush into the
gummy stuff and begin to spread it around on the possum's back.

Last week I roughed her out, paying no attention to
her. Now I glance at her casually, letting my eyes slide
over her affectionately: a sweet mother, a sweet musty
thing with fleas, expecting thirteen teardrop-sized
babies. Her sides flatten out, her nose slopes toward a
rind. This leg reaches out, this hip moves to balance
the weight; straggly hair grows out of the shoulders;

the eyes seem to blink nervously; long teeth protrude
from the deep gash of her open mouth. She squashes
her opposable thumb into a vacant anthill.

Hating to stop even for a minute now that the flow is
going, I bite the wax off my fingers and wait for the pot
to reheat. She is doing all right.

It is so obsessively slow in the doing. Like a crawl of
lava, with infinite delay, the wax builds up into a
brown shape. But the pull between what I'm working
for and what the accruing layers show is the pleasure.

Clay worked so fast. The clay figure, if it turns out as
you want, is at best a suggestion. With the wax you
work against more—have more traction, overcome
more gravity, raise more dust—but this greater work
makes a greater refinement. It takes bleeding out the
armpits, as Locke would put it.

Back into the sticky pan goes the brush, to bring a
new sediment of wax for the possum. It is easy to understand the lure of working against an even greater
push, of working wood or stone or the large unyielding
hunks of metal Locke uses. Chiseling against the grain
of marble: that would be a place to begin!

"So."

I turn and he is right there.

"That's good," he says.

"You're getting easy to please."

"True. I must revive the Socratic method. Where

does she live? How many fleas on her tail?" He grins
at me.

I ask him, "What happens after she is finished? Is it a
ceremony to take her to the foundry?"

"Everything is a ceremony. Which means money is
necessary. First we pack her in aggregate: that stuff
there in the boxes. We mix it with water. Here, I'll
show you."

"My three-year-old makes concrete out of sand and
little chunks of rock."

"Your three-year-old is already four, remember?"

"In here I forget."

He looks at me a minute.

I go back to the lesson. "So we pack her?"

"In a box, careful not to knock the sprues off."

"What are sprues?"

"Little pipes that the stuff goes around so that the
wax will have someplace to run out when it melts and
the bronze will have someplace to run into. *Could* that
be *clearer?*"

"Why doesn't the bronze run right on out, too?"

He wrinkles his face. "Judas, trying to answer ques-
tions. After four hundred times of doing it I ought to
see. . . . You turn it upside down, of course."

"Can I watch?"

"Yes, Cellini."

"You told me his furnace or oven blew up."

"People who remember every word you say." His
voice is softer.

"Help me with this, Locke."

We stand there side by side and he looks. Finally he says, "You don't want to do much more. The rougher the better, especially back here by the tail: that's good enough just like that. It makes a nice vessel. Maybe turn the nose a little, along here. Just sharpen the bridge of the nose and turn it."

"Yes."

One more time I warm the wax. He is right, of course, and my friend comes out of the woods to step in the water pan before our delighted eyes.

CHAPTER

{ 14 }

ARCH and Jeb are in the tree having an argument. Cal and Clyde help me water the back yard. It is a steamy four o'clock.

"Mother, didn't Dad say that some of the oldest rocks in the world are lying around on the ground all over these hills? Just lying around?"

"Maybe he did. I know we are sort of on the old roots of a mountain range that used to be on the edge of a sea. That would be a long time ago." I picture the fault raised up into mountains.

But Jeb isn't satisfied with that. He insists, "My mother said that we used to be under an ocean *right here.*"

I tilt the fault and let the hills fill with sea water.

"Maybe she's right. Although I thought the Permian Sea was farther west. We *are* on the edge of a fault here, hung on the spring-fed edge."

He insists, "My mother said this used to be an ocean."

"Well, if that's right, then the oldest rocks must have been on the bottom of your ocean, because my dad said—"

Cal and Clyde freeze.

"Mama!" whispers Cal.

A large brown rabbit stands *in the yard*.

Clyde lies low, hugging the ground, his ears flattened.

The rabbit in the grass hops to the pan of birdseed on the ground and begins to eat, in a wrinkly, very slow way, mouthfuls of seeds. His high hind legs straddle the pan.

He looks up at us, straight *at* us, then wrinkles back at the sunflower seeds.

It is incredible for him to be here: at four o'clock in the afternoon. How does he know we don't have legions of dogs? How does he know that our pacifist of a black cat is going to lie down by the hose?

"Mama!" Cal's face is shining with delight.

We sit softly on the stiff grass and watch with the older boys.

Anslow coming up the drive to the back yard finds us silent.

"An! This is two surprises. How come you're home

early? Look." I point to the brown rabbit. "Don't startle him. Come sit down with us."

His face looks worried and drawn.

"Anslow?"

"Come in the house a minute."

"Cal, you watch the rabbit for me. Don't move."

We sit in the library and I know something is wrong.

"Clara . . . sweetheart, I have some bad news." Anslow reaches for my hand.

"On campus?"

He looks at me, then looks away. "No." His voice is strained.

I know by his face it isn't good. "What?"

He speaks slowly, holding my hand tightly. "Your mother."

My voice is a whisper. "Tell me."

He is haggard and his silence hits me with it before his words. "She—" He falters and tries again. "She died. Of what they think was a stroke."

In the space of time that I hear it a picture of a freckled face composes itself behind my eyes. Her round Alabama voice says: *Be in the world as if you were a stranger or traveller; when evening comes expect not the morning; when morning comes expect not the evening.*

I try to say something but there is nothing to say.

"Clara? Are you going to be all right?" He gets up and sits down again, trying to put his arm around me. His hands are cold.

I think about it. "No."

He looks at my face closely. "Don't you want to lie down or something?"

But I shake my head, wondering about Daddy. "Do I need to call Daddy?"

Anslow looks uncertain. "If you like. I'm not sure if he . . . if they've decided about all the arrangements."

I have to ask one more thing. "Who called you?"

He whitens and takes a breath. "He did."

I am the rabbit in the grass . . . It makes a chill over me. "An?"

"What, sweetheart?"

"That rabbit—"

"Never mind about that."

"Let me go back outside."

He thinks I mean about the children. "Don't you want *me* to tell the boys?"

"Yes. Yes, please. Bring them in and leave me out a little while. Can you stay here? Do you have to go back to school? Can you see that Jeb gets home? Can you—"

"Of course. Don't think about all that." He looks stricken as I pull my hand loose. "Are you sure you want to go back outside?"

"Please."

Trying to cope with the shock, I watch the rabbit eat. When her own mother died, Mother wrote out a poem that she loved, something of e. e. cummings's, I think, and said it until she learned it:

if there are any heavens my mother will (all by her-
*   self) have*
one. It will not be a pansy heaven
nor a fragile heaven of lilies-of-the-valley but
it will be a heaven of blackred roses . . .

But I forget the rest. It pleased Daddy because he thought Mother was imagining her mother gone to heaven in his garden. What a vast expanse of ego.

But Mother did not see herself as she saw her mother. She thought of her mother as a vivid woman who acted when she thought it was time to act, helping the blacks before it was in fashion, beyond what was required by conscience, and in spite of the leisurely resistance of the South. She liked to get things done in her own style.

My mother thought of herself as slipping in and out of the world, with no public face, as a part of all that moved. *Like wind I come; like water I go . . .*

So now she eats in my back yard, if I can put it like an allegory, rabbit. Or sits forever in the chair in the center of the galaxies of smells that is the garden: with pale translucent skin through which small blue veins are visible, her hair wrapping around her head endlessly, gray threading in and out of the brown.

I don't cry because I see her too sharply. I turn onto my stomach and bury my dry eyes in the prickly Saint Augustine. *You are also the grass.*

CHAPTER

THEY are all asleep and it is finally three in the morning, and cool. The smell of white flowers is in the
moonless air around my bare shoulders.

I am not doing all right.

The boys seemed confused about how they ought
to feel: they made a few tears. Arch said, Gosh, Mother,
and Cal said, I'm sorry, Mama. Anslow wore me all
evening tucked under his arm while he did the phone
calls and began the routine arrangements.

Somewhere back twenty-four years is a young woman
with brown hair and a round voice whose lap I ran to,
whose slim arms I clung to, that I loved . . .

It isn't easy to go back to the faded water colors of
being eight years old.

Half of my childhood summers I spent in Tennessee with the Callisons. My grandmother kept the Red Front store, the church, and her help all under control. Biscuits were always rising near the stove. My grandfather (who got up at dawn to feed the mourning doves on the wide back porch that looked away from Mount Henry to the muddy Mississippi) took me on foot to explore caves used by runaway slaves, thickets of blackberries, meadows of goldenrod, cemeteries with small uniform stones to infants lost in the epidemic. Once we drove his old Ford up to the top of Mount Henry, which is the highest point in Callison County.

The other half of my summers were spent in Alabama with Grandmother Frazier. Here there was less to do: Grandmother and Mother talked all the time and I was left to listen unobserved. Grandmother had many causes. Her favorite quote was a thing I think of Elinor Wylie's:

> *I was being human, born alone;*
> *I am being woman, hard beset;*
> *I live by squeezing from a stone*
> *The little nourishment I get.*

Her house was behind a grove of trees, turned away from the paved street and the smell of paper mills. She was forever telling me that my grandfather had died because the morning made him nervous and the evening made him tired.

My mother was happy in that bare house with its woven Indian rugs, stacks of books, woodcuts. She was happy in the back yard with the sound of cars in the distance. My picture of her there is with an armful of elm and maple branches, her hair caught in the leaves, her face lit from under the pale freckles with a glow. Her Southern voice saying to me, "Honey, it is so good to be *home*."

I wish she were home.

When I am eight I am down at a creek. Down at a creek after a bad fight.

"If you want to write poems, write poems," Daddy had shouted at her. "But not through some correspondence course from the want ads. Couldn't you have asked me? There must be a dozen men on campus who could teach you better than this mail-order instructor. As if there weren't enough mediocrity running loose in the streets. All these sonnet things you've done are about the children you taught in the paper mills of Alabama! Do you wish you were back there, back in that smell? Has the ten years since I came and got you made no impression at all?"

It was their only real fight, but it hurt me in the pit of my stomach.

Down at the creek I looked for crawdads to catch with empty fruit cans. If it was too dry I built small towns with twigs and acorns and pebbles under the shade of the trees.

If there are any heavens my mother will (*all by herself*) *have one....*

Incredibly, as I watch the faded water-color scenes down by the creek, a small furry raccoon straggles up to me.

She is very small and nosy. She peers around the empty pan, where the others fed an hour ago, then stands up slowly on hind legs and looks at me.

Ever so slowly she lowers her paws to the ground and approaches me.

Because it has never happened before—I have never touched one before—because I don't know how to stop her, the raccoon sniffs at my bare toes and my bare knees and my shaking fingers and climbs in my lap.

She is very soft. Her fingers play with the ribbon on my short gown.

"Please!" I beg.

She turns to my begging voice. Her trust is terrifying.

"Go away, stupid little beginning of a bear. Please quit picking at the ribbons of my gown."

She settles down into the nylon lap.

"Don't come out of that—that frame I have around your picture, dumb washing bear. This is no time . . . there is a funeral coming."

She curls in a ball against my stomach. She is very soft.

"Oh, little compromising enemy, *please—*"

Tears stream down my cheeks as I put my hands finally on her furry back and blur all the pictures in the breathing warmth of her coat.

CHAPTER

{ 16 }

SWINGING high above Travis Park, littered with Fourth of July picnic crumbs, in the early sunshine I am putting off going to see Locke. It has been a month without him, and this seems as good a time as any to leave home. Before I got in the car this morning I put on my new delphinium-blue dress. It curves in a long swinging line that I like. My hair is washed and tied with a blue ribbon. Wearing a fresh pink mouth I am admitting how much I want to look like a girl.

June was a tangled month of climbing vines and weeping shrubs under a baking Texas sun. Thistly pink mimosa blooms littered the yard at Arch's school; yellow syrup-smelling retama flowers fell on the grounds at Cal's end-of-school picnic. Down by our creek the air swung with mustang-grape vines, dangling above the drying water.

The funeral itself was unexpectedly bearable in the heavy Alabama morning. Through the open stained-glass windows, over the cloying odor of tube roses, the wind carried the aroma of crape myrtle and paper mills. Rows of old family friends came quietly into the church, wearing hats and gloves. From outside we could hear the small-town sounds of a few cars, a whistle, children. It was like being in Grandmother Frazier's yard.

The minister was a middle-of-the-road Baptist. He was not like the kind we used to hear in Tennessee ranting, "Let us no longer be used as instruments of these twentieth-century pharisees whose preoccupations are but window dressings in the store of life . . ." But neither was he schooled in the language of the new theology like the man at school who gave us Tillich and Buber. This young preacher read the ritual in a soft Southern tone that suggested that he knew that we cared.

It was a comfort to stand in the small church immersed in a tradition of generations of solid believers who had had a clear picture of what is right in the world and who had been willing to stand up and be counted for it. This is a help when you are dealing with the question of what-is-more-than-man.

Cal held my hand. Arch held his grandfather's hand. Anslow stood at my side. What made it bearable was that of course Mother was not there.

The first weeks after the funeral people were very kind.

Some sent food, mostly hams and lemon pies. Daddy wrote from Michigan that he also got lemon pies and that he was working on a theory correlating grief and citric acid. This was very difficult for me to take, but I wrote him every day for a week or so and never asked why the funeral had been in Alabama. I need to believe that it was his way of sending Mother home.

The people that were the easiest to be with were older women, mostly faculty, who had buried so many people, and endured so many bad times themselves, that they knew how to sit around talking about the heat and their grandchildren. They had no need, unlike the younger wives, to prove that they could suffer with me. Their attitude implied that the less one made over death, the more one could endure it.

The day after we got back Hayes brought over a box of chocolates and told me stories about his own mother until I felt that I had known her for years.

I told him about a pair of pawing hound dogs at the home where we stayed in Alabama, and we generalized comfortably that small towns have more dogs than big towns and Southern small towns more dogs than Northern small towns, while Sarah and Anslow complained in low voices about funeral homes.

Sarah took me back to my bedroom, after sending

the boys down to her house for supper, with coffee and a bowl of soup on a tray. But the chocolates looked better than the soup and I ate ten pieces, soft centers and caramels, with my coffee.

The sun came through the curtains, making the yellow room seem on fire. Vases of yellow roses and daisies were on the table under the windows. It seemed all late-afternoon summer sunlight everywhere I looked.

Sarah sat on the end of the bed and talked to me. She said she had thought a lot about her own parents dying and she knew it could make you stop and look at yourself, that seeing what they had done or not done with their lives could be depressing, and she didn't want me to get depressed.

I listened halfway in the pool of sun, finally interrupting her to get her to promise that she would call my teacher and tell him that I wouldn't be there until July. With that promise I rolled over for an after-supper nap.

Evan and Louise came by later that week with scotch instead of chocolates.

Evan helped Anslow drink some of it and told what Anslow thought were funny stories about his experiences probating wills.

Louise visited with me in the kitchen, where I was trying to put together supper. She didn't talk much, or offer to help, which I appreciated.

She asked over her drink, "Were you and your mother close?"

"I think we were."

"You're lucky," she said. "My mother and I weren't too close, and when she died years ago I had an awful guilt feeling, you know? The first months I tried to assure myself I really did remember what she was like, but children never see their parents. Every time we think we're remembering *them* we're only remembering our reactions *to* them."

But I didn't know what to say, and as the meat was ready and the potatoes weren't done we gave the boys a sandwich and took a drink in with the men.

The next afternoon, when I had fallen into a deep before-supper nap, exhausted from listening to people, weary with the effort of responding, sleepless from having sat out most of the night in the yard, Anslow woke me by looking in on me.

"Thought you were asleep," he said. He had something in his arms.

"I'm awake, come in. What is that?"

"Your Mr. Smith brought you this." He showed me a wonderful walnut stump about a foot across and two feet high.

"Is he *here*?" I pulled on my robe.

"He wouldn't stay." He looked uneasy. "I *told* him I'd get you up."

"You told him I was *resting*?"

"You said not to call you for anyone."

"Oh, An!"

"Easy, honey. I didn't mean to upset you. He stayed

only a minute and I did think you were resting." He sat
down on the bed. "He didn't look as I thought he would.
I expected an older, bearded type. He doesn't look much
older than you and he certainly isn't much taller."

"No."

"You're upset?"

"Let me see the wood." He put a stump of smooth
fine-grained wood in my hands. "It's *walnut*." It was
such a kind thing for Locke to do to bring me this, such
a good time for him to bring something that I had
never worked on before. I began to cry.

"His coming has upset you."

"No."

"He said to tell you that neither the armadillo or
your bronze possum was picked for the show." He
watched me worriedly.

"That doesn't *matter*, Anslow."

I got tears on the wood.

Swinging where high-school girls linger, I wish I
could forget all of June. I also wish that I were not
all dressed up in clean sandals and blue hair ribbon to
go tell that man that I think I should leave his carriage
house. That place is my home, and when your mother
dies you need to go *home*.

He is waiting for me at the door. He has on a white shirt and tie. He looks very scrubbed.

He grins at me. "Hello, Clara Blue."

I look at him, very glad to see him. "I brought the walnut. You were good to bring it."

"I saw the three-year-old."

"He's four."

"That's what he told me. He looks like you." There is a pause. "Your husband tell you about the opossum not making the show?"

"Yes. It didn't *matter*."

"Your husband's a very solicitous fellow."

"Did you see Arch?"

"He had a handful of cards or something that he dropped while he was trying to shake my hand. Nice boy. He told me about twenty things about his grandfather. I like that hero worship. It's enough to make you want to be a grandfather."

"Locke?" I stand and look at him.

He looks over my dress and then says, "Time for our cigarette."

We sit together on the edge of a table crusted with dried wax. There is a long silence and I am very aware of him sitting beside me.

"Thank you for the walnut," I tell him again.

He looks away. "Clara, you need to set up a studio of your own."

"I know. On my way over here I stopped at the park to try to get up my nerve to tell you I was leaving."

He puts on his front. "Great minds on a single re-nunciation scene."

But I don't want that. I try to tell him, "Locke . . ."

"What is it?" He is gentle with me.

"Locke, I love you."

He doesn't look at me. "You women think any time you say two sentences to a man that he understands that it's something called love."

"Don't be like that."

He turns to me. "Maybe I need my defense more than you know."

"I am at home with you."

"Home is somebody else's house where you grow up, remember? And you still belong over there at some-body else's house. I met them all. Besides, it isn't me, great as that is for the ego. It's the work you do when you walk through my door. And you can have that wherever you are. When you turn on those hands and make that damn army of raccoons I could be a chair for all you care. That's the thing about you."

"No!"

"If you had your choice between preventing grass stains with me or working on that wood stump you've got there—"

oh god

"—admit that you'd take the mother trapped in that wood."

"Does it have to be a choice?"

"Look at me, will you?"

I look at him.

He speaks very low. "You put my itchy hands on you instead of putting yours on that and you'll wake up at six a.m. tomorrow a culturette."

"*Damn* your theories."

He stands up. "That's better."

I stand up too. "Okay, tell me about the walnut."

"Now?"

"It makes things easier when we are working, and if I'm not coming back I need to learn how to work it. Locke, I can't just walk out the door."

"You have to have a different approach with wood." He turns to find some tools.

With our eyes on the stump we spend the rest of the morning looking at the planes, the lights, and the grain of the wood. Locke shows me a strong rounded torso of a woman, polished and smooth.

As we study my walnut I see a rabbit in it: a rabbit low to the ground with hind legs straddling a pan, a rabbit with ears winged back almost touching his shoulders.

It is our four-o'clock friend who has never come back. It is also something to put my hands on in my own place, my own studio, away from home.

"Here, Locke," I show him. "Can't you see the ears?"

He touches the curve of ears. "Sometimes I think you are born all the time."

CHAPTER

THE phone was ringing when I came in from my last trip to the carriage house, bringing my walnut stump.

It was Anslow who asked, "Did you see the TV?"

"No—"

His voice was jubilant. "He *took* it. He took the Vice-Presidency!"

"Is that good?"

There was a sigh, then his excited voice said, "We're unbeatable."

"I'll go turn it on now."

"They'll probably rerun it all day." He sounded happy. "Hayes asked a bunch of us to come over to-night to have a drink."

"Wives too? I'll get a sitter. I need to get out—"

"Let me meet you there then about seven. Go turn it on."

Tonight he is in the middle of a crowd of excited men.

I am with the wives, all looking festive in hot-pink and loud-orange dresses, who are talking over a tray of Sarah's cheese nachos. We are standing by brass pots of blooming geraniums whose fuzzy leaves have an unpleasant acrid smell.

Moving away from the red flowers I listen to the men as each tells his favorite political allegory.

An is standing on a threshold. He is looking out through an open doorway to the road of the future, leading to machines and possibilities. A heavy gate obstructs the door: it is bad leadership through which we must push, the force of which we must overcome, if we are to climb the pyramid of technological advances which awaits us at the end.

An older man who is wearing a striped tie and a striped shirt is paddling a boat. He is being rushed down the cultural river to the ocean of the future. The current of the river propels him with an unavoidable force—only a Republican would try to paddle the boat against the current.

Hayes is in the midst of the storming of the Bastille, whose one hundred and seventy-first anniversary he is drinking to tonight. His lion's head pretends to wear a cockade hat. Royal troops have withdrawn after the antiquated fort, the almost empty prison, has been stormed by the forces of good on our side. The symbol of freedom has been picked up, tyranny is overthrown, they are licking salt in tricolored hats on the outskirts of a new frontier.

"Clara, you feeling okay?"

Sarah has left the clutch of wives in their bright dresses to rescue me on the edge of the men. Women are nervous when you do not enter into their world (whereas men wish you wouldn't, and that is easier).

I come back with her to the geraniums and wives, but it is difficult to focus on their conversation and I don't keep up with who is talking to whom.

I look around for the large boxer dog, but in vain; he has disappeared, maybe under the couch.

His smooth place on the carpet is occupied by a large woman who says, "As I say, that was the turning point, the single most decisive turning point of the campaign, when West Virginia was forced to look itself in the eye and vote."

Another woman tells her, "*I* had been for him way back when he ran at the convention for Vice President. There I was in Washington, that's how long ago it's been, with the washing machine flooding all over the

floor and diapers everywhere, and we were listening to
the count."

"But I still say that primary—" The large woman
turns for support, "What do you think, Clara?"

Sarah answers for me because I can't find any words.
"That was the day Clara's mother died, the day of the
primary."

This stops their talking for a moment, and then they
are very kind. Realizing that several of them must have
come by with hams and lemon pies, I smile at their
faces and thank them for coming.

A plump girl with a shrill voice asks, "Didn't you just
hate the funeral?"

Without thinking I explain that it was bearable because Mother wasn't there.

They stare at me in embarrassment.

No one says anything.

Sarah passes the tray of nachos, and then they all
begin talking at once about some books they are read-
ing, a quartet of new books. The plump girl has read
them all.

I must have some bourbon to line my stomach against
all their voices. With a mouth full of nachos, cheesy
and hot, I edge toward my host.

He and all the men are talking about some story.
From the looks on their faces it might well be an old
still movie with Charlie Chaplin. It is the story of a
villain called U-2. But it is very complicated and I
can't keep all the subplots straight: there is rioting in

Turkey, overturning in Korea, strain in Africa, rejection in Japan, collapse at the Summit, radios on the floor of the conventions, patterns in the primaries, and a chorus of seven hundred and sixty-one delegates.

I put my glass in Hayes's hand.

"You need a drink," he deduces.

"Thank you. How nice." I am grateful and talk too much. "That's what I wanted. I'll go with you to the kitchen to get it."

He fixes me a strong drink and hands it to me. He says, "It's a great day."

I tell him that we are unbeatable.

He agrees and tells me all about how exactly we are going to win the election. "Democracy in action," he concludes, giving me a hug to emphasize his point. "You look mighty pretty in that blue dress. That a new dress?"

"Yes." Foolish with drink I explain about the dress. "It's because I'm a girl."

He roars back and laughs until his chins shake. "Now honey, there are some things you don't have to go around spelling out."

But I could use a few simple things spelled out for *me* in the midst of all this democracy in action.

At home in the early morning Anslow is still elated.

"What a day!" He lifts me off the floor.

In the dark he says, "That was some party!"

"We can't lose." I whisper to him what he wants to hear.

And as he puts his arms around the girl in his bed it all becomes part of the bright orange and pink, the Bastille Day red-white-and-blue, the room full of voices and the stinging geraniums.

After he rolls over I lie sleepless against my pillow, listening to his even breathing, until it is time to go out and feed my friends in the woods. The dark air is hot and still and I am very lonesome.

CHAPTER

{ 18 }

DADDY is here so I have put my walnut rabbit up for
a while. Clyde is glad; he does not like that damp dripping cave away from the heavy smell of green pecans
and drying sage. He missed the birds.

For weeks I have abandoned him and the boys to
playing Huck-on-a-raft and look-out-for-snakes-by-the-
creek while I opened the grains of the wood and let out
light.

In the middle of the closed-in garage is a dangling
two-hundred-watt bulb above a huge unpainted table
that holds my rabbit, a pot of wax under a piece of
canvas for later, a hot plate where I burn out the bot-
toms of coffee pans.

The rough rock walls hide scorpions and occasional

tarantulas, so I have to wear shoes all the time. The water cooler drips all day: it is like the inside of a limestone cave.

It is impossible, even when the work goes badly, not to admit that it is better having a place at home, because here there is nothing but to work.

My mornings, until Daddy came, were full of pulling the long sloping ears out of their hiding place in the yellow grain of the wood, finding a plane in the wood to make a tucked-in curve for the front feet, a splayed-out arch for the hind legs straddling the water pan, a small bluntness for the wrinkling nose. I love him, eating sunflower seeds all morning.

Once he is under my fingers the work moves in a circle flowing down into the wood and up into my eyes and back into my hands: we make a round curve of work that is smooth like the round curve of the rabbit. While I am there I forget that my arms and shoulders ache from the new resistance of this new medium.

With Daddy here we have the boys all day, and Anslow all evening. Mother has been mentioned only once, when he gave me a sack of letters to her and a few old photographs.

The nicest times are when we swim. Daddy unbuttons his shirt with pigmented hands and dives in— crawling up and down the spring-fed pool—not admitting to himself that he is more winded than he was even on his visit last August, or that it takes longer for him to catch his breath. But he sits on the edge of the pool, palms pressed onto his thighs, head leaning slightly over, catching his breath.

Arch shows off the dives An has taught him; Cal shows that he can swim underwater like a thrashing water beast, coming up only for air. Arch, like his father, is a dolphin in the cold water. Cal, like his grandfather, works too hard and pants and brags about how far he can swim.

I get wet all over and am nowhere else but there, in the pool, in the water, and it is sweet.

Walking with them down to look-out-for-snakes-by-the-creek, Daddy hears about Arch's school.

"And, Grandfather, we learned how many delegates it takes and what the big states are and why they have more electoral votes. I made a chart if you'd like to see it. I still have it. The class got to put on a convention, but some of the kids were absent. Dad said you could tell us how it looked up in Michigan."

And then later, walking back through the heavy humid air, Cal gets his turn.

"Listen, Granddaddy, me and Lee pretend that the earth is too cold. You remember how it was a big ball of fire?"

"I have heard something about that."

"Well, it's too cold and we're going to another planet so far away that if the time didn't get shorter we'd be too old to get there, and we're gonna build a spaceship

and we're not gonna let Mark and David get on because they got all the rocks when we built our sidewalk
and—"

"Wait, stop. You're losing me."

At night, when they have moved to brandy after the
lemon pie, and I have on a fresh dress, maybe my
delphinium-blue, we talk very late in the study.

Archer Anslow Blue and his father-in-law, being
men, have everything in common. Before I married I
thought I could see differences between An's world of
history (based on scientific fact) and Daddy's world of
science (based on historical guesswork). But when
they talk they see the same world.

If it is Anslow's night to talk he may say:

"It may not come to anything, George, but several of
us have been interested in it for some time. It is to be a
special class for the honors program, an interdiscipli-
nary study of the humanities, you might say.

"The kids will have a chance to get a representative
teacher—and we would hope to get one of the better
young men—from each concerned department to teach
his part of the course from the point of view of his
discipline, but tying it into the total framework, the

overall focus. For example, and this is off the top of my head, if we called it something like 'Man's Humanity' someone from the zoo department could lead off and then maybe someone from psychology and then from our department and *we* could have a go at it. You get the idea."

Or if it is Daddy's turn he booms at us while An tamps a careful blend of three tobaccos in his new pipe.

"You already know about it, A.A. There is nothing new to add. It's all a matter of metabolism. Oh, sure, you have to look back at mother and the umbilical cord, and was the head rubbed in the first twenty-four hours and all that popular stuff, but you also have to remember that each person's body has its own differences—in blood function, in excretion—its own poisons and its own beneficial nutrients that are determined at birth and that make a lot more difference than whether the OB that delivered it looked like a father image or not.

"It's all a matter of metabolism; we can be sure that unless the brain takes enough oxygen and burns it at the right rate there will be mental disorder; dementia and diabetic coma testify to that. It's that simple. We think—at least until this last battery of patters we could be pretty sure—that this particular disorder, which the paperbacks call schizophrenia, would show up with a detectable urinary deviation. We've had

some exciting results with this, though. Did I tell you
about the fellow from Japan?"

Tonight they are somewhere in the middle of Arap-
aho sun-rites, and I am trying to remember when I
have been through this before.

"You know, A.A.," Daddy is saying, "they set their
wooden pillars in a circle, with an opening on the east
for the first rays of the rising sun to fall on the dancers.
Same sort of thing as the way the stones were set at
Stonehenge. It's a similar pattern."

"It is, it's a repeat pattern. They can trace solstitial
rites back to the sun worshippers of Neolithic Europe."
Anslow knows about it.

"Reason I brought this up, A.A., is because the
Arapahos have visions: an amazingly large percentage
of cases of what the paperbacks would call schizophrenia occur in connection with these visions, or hal-
lucinations."

Anslow tells it his way. "All I know about their hal-
lucinations, and this is rather interesting, is the fact
that the vision belongs to the person who experiences
it. It's a simple copyright arrangement. For example, if
a wolf in a dream sang you a song, you then own the
song."

I interrupt them. "I *remember*. We talked about
those dreams before, Anslow, and I wondered if the
cave drawings had come to the artists in dreams."

Daddy looks amused and says to me, "Don't I recall

you had some theory that the women stayed home by the fire and painted while the men were out hunting buffalo?"

"Of course they did. Oh, Daddy, don't you remember? An, *you* remember, how funny Mother thought it was when you showed me four sources in three languages proving that they were done by men."

"I don't remember that your mother ever thought anything was funny."

This angers me. "I didn't know you *remembered* Mother."

His voice booms back at me, "Will you expect Anslow to take out your picture after supper every night and shed a few tears?"

"Listen, Daddy, I expect to survive when you are *both* stones facing the rising sun or whatever that was about!"

"Your mother and I got along fine."

"Don't talk to me like that, in that pacifying tone. All I meant—I wasn't going to say one word, but since we got off on this—was, did you *ever* see Mother?"

He wipes his forehead with his lined hands. "Seems like I grew you up with talks about laying the truth out there on the table and no alibis. Don't I recall some speeches along those lines? The truth is I went down to Alabama, into the gummy odor of the paper mills, and took her back with me—a freckled-faced, dedicated teacher. She called her mother and said, 'George came and got me.'" He stares out into space to recapture that trip, but I don't think he can see it any more.

"Daddy, I'm sorry. I'm like Cal saying 'Bad Mama,' saying 'Bad Daddy' to you. I know I don't know any better than you do what she was really like. It's just that I want everybody to see her so she won't just slip away like a rock in the water after the ripples are gone and you can't even tell where it was." There are tears down on my face.

"Come on." Anslow soothes in my direction. "We know it's hard."

Daddy shakes his head: he knows I know it is all too easy.

CHAPTER

SEPTEMBER slips in: thick damp air rising above a patch of bright blue morning glories. The vines, a cousin of the sweet potato, climb up the dry trees in our woods, spilling over onto the caliche path. The jay screams; the mockers rise, scissoring the boundaries of their territory.

Everything has started again. Anslow is fresh and full of man's humanity to man. The boys are in school. I am grinding my stone.

Arch, laden with his new notebook, waits for An. Arch had explained to me about the notebook. "Not that kind, Mother. We had that in second grade. It has to be a loose-leaf with two rings."

Cal is off in a new class, building the spaceship he told Daddy about, with a shoelace of Normally's to pull the release hatch. He tells our new household help all about it. "Lee and I go to school every single day and we get there before Mark and David and—"

Lupe, tiny and silent, nods her head.

She is here to move silently, morosely, taking the breakfast plates covered with egg to the sink. Everywhere she moves she leaves a trail of order behind her. She puts the couch pillows in a row, the magazines in a row, the toothbrushes in a row. This pleases Anslow.

"But Clara," he had said, "you always said help in the house bothered you."

"Did I? It's that I kept using the housework to put off going out there to the garage."

"I guess I understand that. Anyway, we sure can *use* her around here."

"She makes me feel good because she is so cross about it all."

"You're a funny girl."

The first day she came he left a few instructions with her. Every man, I could see, should have several people around he can leave instructions with. Why did I never realize what he was having to do without?

Anslow is running late this morning, is just now tying his tie, because we were up late at Evan's last night with a visitor from the East.

In the damp interior of my home the motor of the fan makes a hum that means I have to work. Cool is coming out its top; hot is coming from the coils of the hotplate warming coffee.

I have added a high stool with rungs that fit my tucked-up feet so that I can sit with my shoes off.

I sent the smoothed, curved rabbit to Locke when I was through. The next day he came with a large quarry stone. He moved the table, cleared a place for the stone, and set up the tools that he brought in a way that satisfied him.

It was good to have his voice and hands in my garage, which became a studio when he entered it. We worked through the morning, concentrating on the stone, until I understood in part how it is shaped.

He left at noon and it was all work. We carefully kept it all work.

This is the first piece I have had to do really on my own. It is the first time I have worked in a medium without seeing pieces of his to go by. He didn't even tell me what sort of things he had done in stone.

It was to have been an armadillo, but as I searched the rock I could see that the figure buried deep inside was an earlier ancestor of the armadillo—a heavy-plated glyptodont.

The shape of the back is uncovered, roughly. I can see where the feet are buried, and the ridges that will go down the back to the nose. He is fossilized, waiting to be excavated by archaeologists here in the damp of this cave.

The resistance of the stone is a joy. It fights against me every grinding, chiseling, pumicing, abrading inch of the way. It is slow beyond imagining and cannot be rolled up for another attempt like clay, or dropped in the warming pan to melt again like wax. It is like the wood: you only have one chance.

The light of the wood was blinding, but the fantastic opacity of the stone is harder yet on the eyes. It swallows light, it swallows motion—it just lies there and you have to quarry it out. I love it.

When the stone threatens to swallow me there is a bowl of marigolds on the back of the table, whose smell I dislike, to keep me anchored in the room.

The stone is like the wood, too, in that you take away everything which is not part of the image. It is just like excavating bones: you must be careful not to chip or break a bone in the digging out, putting in hours of grit and scrape for every inch of exposure. But, like happening upon the bones of earliest man, there is a joy beyond the telling in getting him out intact and perfect.

I work the barest outline of this strange-jointed South American from the Tertiary Period until Cal pulls me off the stool by my legs to come in for lunch. He wants to tell me what his new teacher said.

CHAPTER

AFTER our lunch we take a sticky tour of the hot yard, turning off hoses so the grass won't steam, talking about the shut-tight morning glories, which are taking a nap.

A nap seems like a good idea, and we crawl up on my bed for me to read Cal an afternoon story. Clyde has heard it before, so he puts a paw over his eyes and has a little twitchy dream. Soon Cal can fight his lidding eyes no longer, and he curls up, too.

With them nested beside me, and oppressive heat crowding against the window pane, I shut my eyes.

Yesterday Louise called to ask us to supper. There was an old friend of Evan's in town and they were getting a party together for him. I knew Anslow would

like to go, so I told her we could come. He was pleased
and had me iron a fresh shirt.

Evan gave everybody too many drinks and told what
the men thought were funny stories—at least they
laughed a lot—about illegal election procedures.

He and I talked a little while Louise, lovely in a
black linen dress, flushed her white cheeks at a story
the visitor was telling.

I asked Evan if he thought his friend liked us.

He said, "He thinks we're smashing, but he'll have to
do at least one article mentioning *frontier* and *provin-
cial* of course. No hard feelings." He enjoyed his joke.

"Louise is a good audience for him."

He checked that out. "She is. But it is just an act.
You know, Clara, when I met that blonde in school she
was an actress. I mean the real thing. She worked night
and day painting flats and memorizing scripts. What
hooked me, of course, was that she was all wrapped up
in it: I was lucky to get a kiss and a Coke between
shows. That, and the grease paint on her nose. Men
have a weakness, you know, for women who don't have
time for them. But now she waits for me every night at
the door in her embroidered apron, hoping I'll fly her
to see somebody else's plays."

I tried to picture Louise in an apron, but decided he
was kidding me again. "Are you making that up?"

He squeezed my arm with a soft hand. "Now how
could you think that?"

What I remember clearly about last night was seeing

Louise and one of her daughters standing in a doorway when I went upstairs to find a bathroom.

The plump girl—Daphne or Diana, whichever is dark like her father—was crying inconsolably. She was in short green pajamas with one roller in her straight black hair. Her sallow face was puffy from crying.

Louise tried in vain to calm her. "You can't let it get *to* you like that, sugar. These things are going to happen all your life." She stood watching the girl. "You *can't* let it get to you."

But the girl did not hear.

Looking tired and uncertain, strained around the eyes, Louise shook her head. It was not the gesture she made downstairs that sent thick fair hair falling across her cheek, but just a jerky gesture of frustration. The girl—Daphne?—was years away from her mother in a private teen-age world.

She stared at her daughter and I stared at her. I remembered her saying about her own mother that you never see your parents, you only remember your reaction to them.

When I got back downstairs later, Louise was by the door smiling up between Anslow and the visitor.

Now with my eyes closed I see her standing defeated in the upstairs doorway.

If your husband idealizes you at a moment in your past, and your children are too lost in themselves to know you are there, who is there to see you?

I shift carefully so as not to awaken Cal and reach in

my bedside drawer for the sack of letters to Mother
that Daddy left with me.

I will catch a glimpse of Mother through her friends.

I open the lemon-scented sachet bag, and dump a
small pile of envelopes on the bed.

Here is a packet from a friend of Mother's: a woman
writer that she admired and wrote to for over thirty
years. I open one dated 1935; Mother would have been
thirty.

What are you doing with your offspring in school?
Besides being an audience for George? Thanks for mentioning my new collection. It is doing better than I had a
right to expect. This is a frantic time of year for me. How
about you?

Write again, if you're not too busy copying George's
notes. Always love to hear. Must run—

Lou

There is a smaller packet from the man in Alabama
that Daddy used to say he came and took Mother away
from. The man never married, which seemed romantic
to me. Once or twice visiting Grandmother Frazier we
went to his apartment, which smelled of tobacco, and
the grownups had tea and talked in voices too low for
me to hear. I pull out a letter dated 1955:

Thank you for your kindly letter to a lonely old man.

Imagine my surprise that you had heard about my illness.

This stint in the hospital has been longer than I expected, although as you may know I have not been entirely well and myself for a number of years now. I am grateful that the bank has generously once again allowed me sick leave.

How is your attractive and now fully grown daughter? A fine lady no doubt by this time, and supplying you with grandchildren perhaps.

We all share with you your loss occasioned by the death of your mother. She was an unusual woman, as no one is more aware than yourself, having lived under her care.

Again my thanks for your solicitude,

Frank

There are others. There is even a small bundle from me. The first is a letter I must have written from Tennessee on a summer visit. She would have been—I count up slowly—thirty-eight, and I, fifteen.

Everybody here is so proud of Daddy's new book! Grandmother has it out on the table in the parlor to show to everybody who comes!

Grandfather and I feed the birds every day when the sun comes up. He looks so much older, and Mount Henry so much smaller, than I remembered from two years ago!

Please write me longer letters. I love you.

Here are some from my father. Did he know they were in here? It is hard to make myself open one. At last I pick out the oldest, at least the most yellowed, one.

I can't wait forever. I know it isn't that anemic bank clerk that keeps you there. Make up your mind between teaching those rednecks and raising my sons.

I'll be down Friday.

George

Among the letters are scraps of paper on which she has noted her meditations in tiny handwriting:

When it comes, you will be prepared.
Observe in yourself what is already there.
The red bird calls, the star burns, without . . .

I can read no more.

She is not anywhere in the letters. These people and the heat outside have turned her to vapor, to steam. I focus fiercely on her picture in the garden until my eyes get wet and my hands cover my face and I like Clyde have a twitchy dream.

Arch wakes us to tell us what his new teacher did.

CHAPTER

{ 21 }

LATE at night I come out to play a little ribbon game in the yard. My friend distracts me as I try to think about the quarry stone and then about Mother's letters.

He is foolish and does not tire of playing in the sweet hot air beside the blue, just-opening morning glories. He is so sweet maybe this would be a good time to share him with the boys. They might like to *see* me once, playing a ribbon game.

They are excited to be waked up in the night, and as they trail along behind me in the dark I explain about him. "Are you listening?"

"Yeah, I guess so." Arch in his pajamas stares at me

sleepily. "Is that all you wear out here? That gown thing? Good grief!"

I rough his hair.

"Mama, you said there was a raccoon, but I don't see him." Cal is walking around and around looking in the pitch black under every tree. There are probably forty snakes beneath the sumac waiting for his fat legs. I lost my mind bringing them out in the middle of the night.

Cal pulls at my arm. "Mama!"

"Is that him, Mom? He's gonna—good grief!" My friend is pulling on the buttons of Arch's pajamas.

Cal lies down on his stomach beside the raccoon, who puts his nose against Cal's. They are eyeball to eyeball. "I love you, raccoon," Cal tells him in a loud whisper.

"How come this one's so friendly, Mom?"

"I don't know."

"Can I take him to school? You know maybe just catch him one night, in one of those cages that doesn't hurt them and take him to school?"

"No."

"I knew you'd say that. Okay, can I take his picture? We could get some flashbulbs. Can I?"

"Why do you always have to have something to take to school to show? Why can't you just watch him now?"

"Listen," Cal whispers. "I love you." The raccoon

walks up and down his back, plays with his bare feet.

Arch tries to explain to me. "People just don't go to the South Pole or the moon or somewhere and come back and say, 'You know what I saw?' They bring pictures and samples and things. You have to have some thing to prove that you saw it. Gosh, those kids wouldn't just believe what I saw if I just *said* I saw it."

"But why do you have to *tell* all those kids?"

"There's no point in just seeing it if you're not going to tell somebody about it; if you're not going to tell the guys—" He groans with the effort of trying to get through to me.

"That must be how it is with your dad."

"Well, can I? Take his picture? Next time?"

"Sure, why not?"

"Great! If you could pay for the flashbulbs I could take my money and get the film. Which is more, flashbulbs or film?"

The animal is on top of Cal's head, playing with his hair. Cal is laughing and squirming in the grass in the middle of the night.

"I could get him eating, maybe. Would he eat out of your hand, Mom? And climbing around on Cal?"

"Okay, wildlife photographer, let's go in. There are one million snakes waiting for your brother out here. Come on, Cal." I lift off the funny, nosy buddy.

"See you, raccoon!" Cal whispers.

"Gee, that was really great." Arch pats the top of the raccoon's head.

Sleepy and sticky we leave the smell of green pecans and crawl back into our beds.

It was nice of the boys to let me see them with the raccoon.

CHAPTER

{ 22 }

FLOODS of unexpected rain wake me. It is a crashing, soaking storm. Fat Clyde is nested between my knees with his paw over his eyes. Beside me Anslow is deep asleep, an arm flung over his eyes.

Water is everything.

I watch the long gray sheets beat the pecan branches over and over against the windows; watch the gray hills emerge from wraps of fog through the rain.

Sometimes when it rains I pretend it is drenching the trees all around the state. I start here in the cedar brakes and go west to the spring-fed Edwards Plateau, nourishing the great weeping cypress and hard woods and farther west to the blue-green juniper in the Big Bend, and up through the dry stretches of ocotillo and lechigillo, out to the western reaches, feeding the ponderosa pine, then north to the waving buffalo grasses of the panhandle.

I imagine the rain in sheets of water coming east down through sparse thirsty mesquite and scrub oak, down into the tall scented pine forests banding the state, and on south, soaking palmettos and flooding the salt grasses that hug the humid coast, and, in rivers of rain, swinging back through the brush country into the irrigated troughs of valley citrus and palms.

It is good to pretend we are quenching the droughts, raising the underground water, feeding springs and rising streams, and that the whole state will never be thirsty again.

A sleepy voice near my face asks, "Raining?"

"Flooding."

"Sounds good."

It is pleasant to be in bed awake in the same part of the morning.

He rolls over. "I ought to get up."

"Listen to it."

"I never get used to finding you still in bed when it rains."

"If we lived in the monsoons I would never get up."

"What time is it?" he asks, hunting for his watch.

He checks and then remembers, "The paper must be soaked."

I tell him, "The paper this morning will say that we are unbeatable, that we have all the states sewed up tight." I smile over my pulled-up covers.

"That's what I want to read, all right." He pats in my direction, disturbing the cat.

After a minute Anslow offers, "I guess it's my turn to say that this area is becoming a desert."

"An, I wasn't going to say that."

"You are an open book. You're looking out that window counting every cactus in the state, aren't you?"

"Sort of."

"I ought to get up."

"An, I had a happy dream—"

Cal throws himself on our bed. "Is it today you're going to make my werewolf suit? Listen, it's almost Halloween."

"Mom? Aren't you all *ever* gonna get up? The clock says it's seven fifteen. We'll be late." He is wild with anxiety and sleep in his unbuttoned pajamas.

The boys do not like any deviation in schedule: eggs at seven thirty are terrifying if you are used to eggs at seven fifteen.

An tells them, "Relax. We're getting up this minute. If someone would move off my leg." He tousels Cal's hair. Boys must have twenty-thousand head roughs by the time they are grown: it is the one universal gesture of affection to boys. I wonder if this is why men hate to get bald? Nobody pats a naked head.

I reach out my stubby hand and pat a bare head.

"Hey!" he says, but he likes it. "Scram, boys, and we'll get dressed." As they disappear he says, "You're very nice this morning; let's move to the monsoons."

I rub his head and get a kiss. He has been very kind with me since Daddy was here. The cat moves to the floor, grumbling.

I dreamed of a wonderful bear with paws spread out in the round circle of a hug, open in front of his chest. Unlike real bears, his face was smiling and trusting. I wanted to give him the big hug he was expecting. He needs to be done in bronze, shiny bronze, and I am sick of grinding away stone. Sick of working so long and endlessly on that heavy plodding stone glyptodont who roams the rain forests trampling ferns that will never grow again, falling into swamps, sucking insects with a sound that there are no human ears to hear. Besides, with his bad hearing, he can never find his female in the breeding season in all the undergrowth and they will all die out.

Last week I shipped him off to Locke, sick of the sight and weight of him, but now, out the window, while Anslow shaves, I see the glyp rooting for grub in the pouring-down rain.

It is wonderful to be chewing on the oil-field wax again, filling my head with the taste, wonderful to roll the sticky ball in my hand and stand it up into a massive bear. I had to sweep away layers of stone dust that covered the floor, and hose it off, but there is still dust in the air.

There is a cushion on my stool, a wastebasket, a bend-neck table lamp, and, today, a vast pot of yellow chrysanthemums propping open the door. Now that it is cooler I can leave the door open for Clyde and the breeze to come in and out.

Sarah comes into the studio followed by the scent of rain.

"Lupe said it was all right for me to come?" She makes it a question.

I tell her it is fine, that I am glad for a chance to stop working. Pulling my mind off the bear, I light the burner under the coffee.

She asks, "What are you making this morning?"

I show her the bear, or rather the rough shape that is going to be a bear. It needs to lean forward more. And the shoulders need to slope more.

She comes over to look at him, and it bothers me when she lightly touches his coat. "Didn't you say that you were through with wax? You told Hayes and me that the harder your medium was to work against the more you liked it."

"Did I? Why do people always remember something you said some other day?"

"But you said that."

I tell her, "Today I like wax." We have our coffee and I ask, "How is baby Jackson?"

"When I left he was back to pulling all the socks out of Hayes's drawer. He can stand at exactly that height."

"Doesn't it seem strange to have Cal and Lee gone every morning?"

She agrees. "Have you *seen* the corner of that school-room? They have stacked all the wood crates that are supposed to be parts of a playhouse into a spaceship. She let them put a chair in there, and spools and I don't know what all."

"You don't think Mark and David will get to Mars first?"

She laughs and looks restlessly around. "What did you do with the stone dinosaur?"

"Sent it off to Mr. Smith."

"Does he still place your things? That's nice."

I change the subject. "Anslow says Hayes is doing a wonderful job with the history part of the marathon humanities course."

"He sure works on it all the time, which means he still hasn't touched his book."

I smile, thinking of the people in his book.

She sighs. "He does love being in front of two hundred students, with charts on the chalk-board he can explain. I even went to listen to him the first day. But at home he is still the same old Hayes. We get in such a

routine, I can't tell one day from the last. At night
mealtime has to be a chance for the boys to say two
words to their daddy without fighting. Then we try to
have a quiet spell after supper. But at the table the
boys *always* say the same things, and after supper I
always tell him the same things." She looks at me ear-
nestly. "You can only laugh about Normally so many
times."

I don't know what to say.

She goes on, "I used to think that vacations were a
change, that suddenly in a new environment you
would look at each other in a new light. But now that
we go camping we each have a set chore, except Baby
Jackson, who finds something new to eat off the ground
at each place, and it is just the same whether we are in
Big Bend or the Big Sandy."

I look at the shoulders of my bear and then back to
her sturdy troubled face. "You're not pregnant?"

"That's all we need: Light Horse Harry, the fourth
boy." She laughs. "I'm not. I'm just in a rut."

I can picture big Hayes troubled by her restless-
ness, picture him setting deep into his chair and listening with wrinkles on his brow. I ask, "What does Hayes
say?"

"I tried to talk to him about how I feel, but you
know men. He says, 'Do whatever you want to do,
honey,' and then asks me for the tenth time if I think
Jeb is getting out of hand, or Lee is going to need

braces, or if Jackson will be trained by Thanksgiving."
She puts her chin in her hands and begins to cry.

"Gosh, Sarah." I pour her some hot coffee.

"Sorry." She wipes her nose. "Funny how you never realize the shape you're in until you start talking. I thought I was fine when I left; I was just coming over to say hello after the rain."

Lupe interrupts to let me know she has been bothered by the telephone.

It is *Locke.*

"Say, lady, you want to make a raccoon?"

"Locke." My face gets red. It is good to hear his voice.

"I found a pedestal for your glyp."

"Where?"

"Middle-sized show. You got the purchase prize, which means two hundred dollars and your name in lights."

"Is that true?"

"If you can believe the judges." He hesitates. "What are you working on?" And for a minute it is his real voice.

"A bronze bear for you to melt out."

"I'll work you into my schedule." He has back his defense. "Sold my welded figure, the latest, and am going down to Houston this week with her. But I'll be back in time for the grand opening of your show."

"When is it?"

He tells me all the details.

"Locke, thank you."

"Don't thank me, thank the judges." And he is gone.

Sarah is dry-eyed and composed again, and waiting to talk.

I tell her about the glyp and the prize.

"Clara, how grand. We'll have a party!" She looks delighted. "Will it be at the museum?"

I am not sure, but I nod.

"That's marvelous for you, but look at me, Clara, here I go again, planning a party at four hundred miles an hour to give me something new to do."

She stands up and shakes her head. "Did you ever notice, Clara, that as soon as you begin looking at your navel and panicking there is always someone coming to town or leaving or having a baby that needs a luncheon or shower or party? Women must have devised their social life as a prevention for madness! I will find myself wondering how someone is doing whom I haven't seen for months and making plans to get together as if that were of major importance. . . . Well, that *is* exciting news. Did you call Anslow?"

"Not yet."

"He should be proud of you."

I tell her that he is very kind about my work.

"Tell him that I said a party, and that you deserve a new dress. Now I am going to take my introspection home and get that boy out of the socks. Let Arch come down and play with Jeb this afternoon: they can dam the creek." At the door she says, "Sorry I was such a goose."

"I'm glad you were here when he called," I say, and it is true. "It isn't easy to share things with Lupe."

"I never think of *you* needing to share." She starts down the street.

I must call An, and I do—after working the shoulders of the bear into one smooth downward slope that curves into a hug—but by then Anslow has gone to lunch.

When I finally tell him, it is over our drink before dinner. I went out and bought a dress to celebrate, a dress to wear for the glyp (and his friend when he drives up from Houston), and I am wearing it.

Getting the dress was a problem. My blue had been so easy, but I couldn't find another color that wasn't blue.

The lady showed me geranium red, and tomato red, and redbud red, until I had to tell her that I didn't like red. She asked what colors I did like, and what colors I wore—but I couldn't remember anything but blue jeans and my delphinium.

I tried on some practical browns, and some yellows with fat rounded flowers, and some more with cramped bunchy flowers, and lots of pastels with buttons and collars and gathers.

As I was about to leave my eyes saw a gray and white, a really sweet gray and white, that was soft to the touch and bare-armed. It had a white curve at the throat and a wide white band down its length. The rest was a rough slate gray that the lady said was silk.

It cost half as much as my glyp and I bought it.

Anslow likes it. "Another new dress? It looks nice on you."

"It's to celebrate."

"Good. I'll get us a drink in front of the news. Let me put these quizzes up."

"An—I'm trying to *tell* you. You don't like it when you hear these things later in front of other people."

"That's an ominous beginning if I ever heard one." He smiles and waits.

I tell it very fast. "Locke called and said that my glyptodont had won the two-hundred-dollar purchase prize in a show."

"Why, sweetheart, that's great. *Isn't* it?" He gives me a kiss. He smooths back his straggling hair and assumes a hearty voice. "The lady in the gray dress is my wife, the sculptress. Hold your applause, please."

CHAPTER

{ 23 }

LINGERING at Travis Park on the way to the glyp's party I swing up into the clear fall air, my feet higher than my head.

Across the stretch of deserted park all the leaves that turn in Texas have turned to dusty yellow, brown-red and rust. It looks like a hedge of smoldering fire on the edges of the cold dry creek. It looks like fall in Alabama.

I am catching my breath before diving into all those people. That massive wax bear is good to think about. He has such a reach he could squeeze you out of existence in a fit of love if you got inside those fur-coated arms with their deadly unretracted claws. He is ready to cast, and I love him. But I always love them at this stage.

Yesterday I went to see the glyp on his pedestal. He was on a wood table that should have held a lamp, set against a white stretch of wall with his backside to the people who drifted in the door. I had dreaded seeing him stumbling along in public out of the studio; with his bad hearing and bad eyesight and plodding feet he looked as if he might plow into the wall at any moment.

I had been terrified he would look different off my table away from the damp and the scorpions, but he had a haze of fern forest all around him. He had a hot humid shell of air that stayed with him and he looked just the same. His plated stony back seemed a heavy load to carry around the length of South America. No wonder his descendants got smaller and grew paper shells.

"Very nice," I had whispered to the glyp.

I don't want to go back today and see him with lots of people there and me having to scissor around in this gray-and-white-stripe of dress saying the right things to people who are looking at him.

Dreading that scene, I do not see Locke until he speaks.

"So," he says. "Hiding out here."

"Locke!" It is good to see him; he is very scrubbed in his white shirt and tie. "Did you come here to find me?"

"I did. I drove back from Houston and washed my pits and knotted this tie to get to the Museum in time to see you receive the masses. And there the masses are, and *here* you are."

"You've already been there?"

"I have. You know, it isn't being a culturette to go and let the public pick at the hem of your dress. It's being grateful that they have that much sense."

"Ugh."

"Who needs people who play hard to get?"

"Am I?"

"What do you call this swing bit?"

"Locke, did you see the glyp, facing the wall?"

"I put him there myself two days ago."

"He isn't mail-order, is he, Locke? He isn't corre-spondence-course, *is* he? He is *good*, isn't he?"

"He is. But you have to get up at dawn every morn-ing and ask that. You go to bed thinking you made the Venus de Milo with three arms and you come in in the morning and there is a twenty-five-cent plaster-of-paris penny bank. Every day you have to fight the mail-order bit; it never gets any easier. So don't let this good piece go to your head."

"But you have to see a good one once in a while to be able to keep working, don't you?"

"You have to watch the people look at a good one. Now."

I think about that. "When you were there were there many people?"

"Lots of them. Hundreds. Maybe twenty. And your

husband, that solicitous fellow, was pacing back and forth."

"Anslow is there?"

"He was relighting his pipe, looking at the door, walking back and forth like someone was having a baby in the next room."

He won't understand that I am not there. "I didn't know he would be there."

"You're an egotist, Clara Blue, an insufferable self-centered egotist."

"It's true."

"Climb in my car and I'll take you over there."

"All right, Teacher."

He grins at me. "I've waited a long time for you to say that."

I look once more at the creek rimmed with fall leaves, seeing a walnut face that I might make framed with branches of sumac and tallow trees.

Inside the museum I see Anslow across the long stretch of polished floor. He is working a toothpick or something down into his pipe and talking to Sarah.

Locke puts a weight of programs into my hands, but they fall all over the floor as I run and fling myself at Anslow's chest, bumping into people on the way.

"Sweetheart!" He is relieved to see me.

"An, I'm sorry."

"Where were you? We called and Lupe didn't have any idea."

"I got cold feet, and Locke came and got me down at the park."

"Good thing *someone* knew where to find you." Anslow looks around, hurt, but Locke has disappeared.

I ask An, "Did you see the glyp over there?" He is still in his haze, turned toward the wall.

"We've gotten well acquainted by now."

"He isn't mail-order, is he? He isn't correspondence-course, *is* he, An?"

He reaches around my shoulder reassuringly. "Of course not, sweetheart. He's the best thing in the show." We look at him. "By the way," he says, "the prize is mentioned in the program, but they don't have anything on him. I thought there might be a ribbon."

"He'd step on it."

"*He*? I wonder if the men in the world appreciate this recognition?" He looks happy. "You were cute," he says, "when you came running across the floor, dropping the programs. It was like old times."

We stand together—him thinking of times by the goldfish pond, me thinking of the glyp in the rain forest —and listen to all the people.

They are excited, and kind, and ask about the stone, and the prize, and how Anslow likes having his wife busy all the time, and if we want some more of Sarah's special punch.

It is a party; we drink to a long life and many happy returns for the glyp.

CHAPTER

{ 24 }

BUT while the stone glyptodont made his debut in the twentieth century, the rest of the country was electing a President.

In return for my celebration this morning we invited people over to celebrate tonight the sweeping victory of Anslow's candidate.

In the early morning hours, however, the picture looks increasingly gloomy to the crowd of men who are discussing with Anslow whether we are seeing the last of the past or the first of the future in the results of the election.

Faced with the possibility of defeat, they are reconsidering the allegories they fashioned in the glow of the July convention:

It looks to Hayes now as if the Royalists might re-take the Bastille.

It looks to the man in the striped tie and striped shirt as if the Republicans might be changing the course of the river.

To Anslow, standing on the threshold, it looks as if a heavy gate is swinging shut on the doorway to tomorrow.

A lot of scotch helps the time crawl by as the returns seesaw in and IBM analyzes the returns and the men analyze how the computer figures it out. From where I stand, with the wives, wondering if it is late enough for my friends to be out looking for food, the men's voices sound indistinguishable and worried.

"But I thought we fought all this out back in the primaries. Back in West Virginia."

"That image faded. Maybe if he had met it head-on again?"

"Man, I thought the day he agreed to become Vice President we had it made."

"Remember that? We thought it was in the bag."

"It's got to be all right. You guys are the original pessimists. Look at Connecticut."

"And South Carolina. That was pretty."

"We couldn't do it without Illinois, that's who."

"Would you quit sounding like it was sewed up? We'll wake up tomorrow and find—"

"Who's going to sleep?"

"You have to remember things will look different the later it gets."

"Worse is what they always look the later it gets. Beautiful is what it was supposed to have been before midnight."

"How about that cheery IBM one-hundred-to-one-against for openers?"

"What I need is another drink."

"If we don't go home Anslow isn't going to have anything left but ginger ale."

While they talk each of the wives tells how her husband grasps the myriad factors that go into a national election.

A plump girl that I have seen before is quoting a British weekly as Sarah and I slip off to make coffee.

Hayes and Anslow come in, with empty glasses, asking for scrambled eggs and bacon.

Anslow looks exhausted. He was keyed up all day long, and now his body sags under this additional strain. He leans against the counter and takes off his tie.

Hayes is red-faced and short of breath. His shirt is wrinkled and he looks worn out. He gives me a halfway hug.

Sarah looks for another can of coffee, which we finally find behind the birdseed.

Hayes makes an effort at conversation. "Sarah tells me you packed them into the museum this morning."

"I haven't thanked her for the party."

Sarah reaches for the eggs. "We're even; this party is going to last all night."

I tell Hayes, "You look gloomy."

He wrinkles his big forehead. "Things aren't going quite as well as I expected tonight. I'm afraid I got my hopes real high. But I do have some news for you, Clara."

I smile at him. He finds it hard to stay discouraged for very long. "We need some good news."

"At last the battle is over," he says. "The ravine is full of the butchered dead, and the general is off reconnoitering the situation, as the newscasters would say." He beams at me.

I can't believe this. "He is *out of the tent*?"

"You want to drink to it?" He fills his glass.

"Marthanne?"

"That girl finally got hers under the covered bridge. She may well be on her way to twins by now. Twins run in the family."

I grab his big arm. "But Hayes—!"

"Facts of life."

"But Hayes, I didn't want him to leave the tent. I wanted it like it *was*."

Hayes laughs. "A conservative in our midst! You better keep your voice down."

Anslow scolds lightly, "Take it easy, Clara. Hayes may need that arm again someday."

And Sarah says, "I thought I told you. After almost a year of moving pins around on the map he is finally getting it down on paper. Every night I have to type up his notes." She looks delighted.

I turn away and stare at the skillet full of scrambling eggs.

It is tomorrow when we climb into bed.

The squeeze of the election shows in Anslow's tired voice. "I had no idea it would go so close."

"But we won."

He lets that soak in as we undress. "If that's certain, that's what counts." He stretches out. "That's what counts, all right."

"You'll be excited when you've had some sleep."

"It was sure close." We lie in the dark thinking about it. Then he says, "You should be excited yourself after seeing the stone animal you did in the show this morning."

"You were nice, An, to come down to the museum. I thought you would be in class."

"You know, Clara, I had looked forward to that. I had thought, in my simple way, that when you had it displayed in the show you would understand how it

was about my book. My thinking was that maybe you
didn't understand because you had never produced
anything yourself."

"You gave me the clay." I need to thank him.

But he is trying to explain. "It was the same for you
when it was your *own* show, wasn't it? That's the fact I
can't get used to. You didn't care about seeing him
displayed at all, did you?"

"I did."

"Or about the prize either, did you?"

"I *did*."

"What got the biggest rise out of you all day? Not
your show, or the election of the President, but that
Hayes finally got started on his book."

"But I want to picture the general in his tent."

"You should be glad for Hayes that he is getting that
show on the road after years of procrastinating."

"But it was a comfort to think of him in there."

He states in a tired voice, "You want things out there
where you can look at them from a safe distance and
not get involved."

"It's true." How can I explain that when you have *no
shell at all* there are enough things that come right up
and get under your skin—climb in your lap and play
ribbon games, change every day like your sons, who
still care a lot about a lot of things, look at you with
light eyes, so that you don't have to look for things to
get involved in. "An, it's just that I need some things to

stay the same. I need to picture Sarah always in brown and pink; Marthanne always on the bridge; the glyp never extinct in the ferns; the raccoons begging by the feeder tray; the armadillo in the grass; my mother in the garden . . ."

He sighs. "Life isn't like that." Reaching out his hand, he says, "I have got to accept the fact that we are not *ever* going to have the same approach."

I hold his hand. "You are married to a conservative, as Hayes said."

"That must be the basic problem." With a short laugh he puts on a soapbox voice. "Can a reactionary from the paper mills find happiness with a liberal—"

"A visionary."

"—from the piney woods?" He laughs as if there was nothing else to do but laugh.

I tighten my hand. "Anslow, I want you always with your feet in the past and your eyes on the future."

He pulls me close. "I want you, too."

I beg, close to his face, "Don't ever change." But, like me, he grows older as the night wears on, older with every breath.

"We couldn't change if we wanted to, sweetheart. We *are* the way we *are*." He holds me tight and says, "And you are a funny girl."

CHAPTER

{ 25 }

THE cold creeps up the ravine carrying the end of the year in its teeth. I am sitting out wrapped in a heavy coat watching the possum eat and smelling the damp cedar thawing in the dawn.

It is good to sit out here. I am inside too much now, for work is all I do, except when An comes home, or the boys beat the door down, or friends come to the studio.

Sarah came yesterday in brown wool slacks and sweater to watch me work up the wax for a weathered-looking bronze I am starting of the general. I am going to do a harried, bearded, worried general who will sit in my cold studio, by the pan of wax and the burned coffee pot and the nest of tarantulas, forever poring over maps while his soldiers crawl up the hilly terrain and Marthanne waits for his aide by the bridge.

Sarah said when she took a cup of coffee, "Any time of day I come over you're out here. You'll wear yourself out if you don't set aside regular hours."

I think about that and explain, "It isn't like that any more. I went to the carriage house at regular times, but now it is turned around and I set aside time for other things that I *have* to do, and am out here on this stool the rest of the time. I'm here unless I can't be here."

"Well, tomorrow you have to be at our house to help us bring in the New Year." She thinks aloud about that. "It's *ring* in the New Year that people say. Maybe I should get bells for everyone. I have candles. You have to see: I have candles all over the house."

Twice my friend Louise has come by.

The last time she came she stood around, in a black-and-white skirt and jacket, smoking and watching me work on the walnut head of Mother I was finishing for Daddy's Christmas.

It had been hard to work on a human face. Hard to grasp the relation of features and bones and expression.

I wished for a chance to study the faces in Locke's studio. But instead I had studied my own in the mirror, peeling off with my eyes down to the bone structure and then layering back muscles, skin, hair, seeing finally the total impression that comes from the look in the eyes, the angle of the head, the smile. I realized that I had never seen myself before.

The head—smoothed, polished, glowing and freckled from yellow lights in the wood—was a present for Daddy to stick behind some stack of books in his study, so that I could think of him caught again in the present instant with Mother.

Louise didn't try to talk but walked around and let me work. After a while she said, "That's good. Do you always concentrate like this?"

"When it's going right. I am slow to get into it."

"It must be fun." She stood by the little heater that fights the dripping cold and looked at the wood. "I don't do anything but pick at the girls."

Remembering an upstairs doorway, I told her honestly, "You do that well."

She looked up quickly, "You're being facetious?"

"No."

She stood with her legs to the heat and finished her cigarette. "You're hard to figure, Clara."

Anslow asked me what Louise and I had talked about.

"Nothing really," I told him, which was true.

"No complaints against your husband?" he asked lightly.

"We didn't talk about you all—or anything much. I just worked."

"I know how she kids around." He gave me a pat on the shoulder. "Have you heard any more about when your dad is getting in for Christmas?"

Locke came by too last week. We were both back in jeans and tennis shoes, not scrubbed up.

His light eyes studied the wood head. "Your mother?"

"They are almost all mothers."

"This *is* her, isn't it?"

"Yes."

"She looks like you."

I watched him study her. "I did her before, in a way. Do you remember the wood rabbit?"

"I remember them all."

After a minute I ask, "How did they like the birds you took to Houston?"

"That's what I came to your lair to tell you." He watched me closely. "I can't fight that adoration down there any longer. It feeds my faltering ego and gives me the strength to work fourteen hours a day instead of the usual twenty-four."

"What does that mean, Locke?"

"Something like this, Clara Blue: that I am moving to Houston."

"No." I looked at him.

He had on his defense. "I'll peddle your pieces on the big market. There's a gallery or five that can be your exclusive outlet. That is, if you ever make one again that you'll let me put somewhere: you keep giving them away."

"But the carriage house?"

"Who needs it?" He said my words to me.

So I said his. "Let's smoke your cigarette."

He sat on the edge of the table facing my stool. There was nothing to say.

I knew of course that it didn't matter about his place here; that he would come crawling out and throw himself at the floor at five a.m. and listen to the sound of the sky hitting the earth wherever he was. Wherever he is all his pieces will be good.

"So," I said at last. "Move to Houston."

He concentrated on the wood. "It needs to be scooped out a little more at the chin, like her face was looking out more. See? Here." He touched the wood and I liked his hand on her still face.

And he was right; it was better.

I have only cried two times because he is leaving, as most of my time there is nothing but to work.

Watching in the cold half-light the possum that I love, I pull my feet under my coat. She does as she has done for centuries: steps in the water pan, trips over rinds, picks at her food with long fingers and sharp incisors.

It is sad that she never makes a new connection, never stumbles onto the possibilities of her opposable thumbs, never changes.

We are not like the possum. There would not be the urgency to capture my pictures forever in wood and stone and bronze if the scene never changed.

It is knowing that no day ever comes again that makes me get up to watch each new dawn light the edges of our woods.

A NOTE ABOUT THE AUTHOR

Shelby Reed Hearon was born in 1931 in Marion, Kentucky, and is descended from a long line of Virginians and Kentuckians (including the first governor of Kentucky, for whom she was named). She grew up in Kentucky, but moved to Texas, where she finished high school, graduated from the University of Texas, and married Robert J. Hearon, Jr., a lawyer who practices in Austin. The Hearons live just outside Austin with their two children—Anne, born in 1956, and a son, Reed, born in 1957. This is Mrs. Hearon's first novel.

A NOTE ON THE TYPE

The text of this book is set in Monticello, a Linotype revival of the original Binny & Ronaldson Roman No. 1, cut by Archibald Binny and cast in 1796 by that Philadelphia type foundry. The face was named Monticello in honor of its use in the monumental fifty-volume *Papers of Thomas Jefferson*, published by Princeton University Press. Monticello is a transitional type design, embodying certain features of Bulmer and Baskerville, but it is a distinguished face in its own right.

Composed, printed, and bound by
The Haddon Craftsmen, Inc., Scranton, Pa.
Typography and binding design by
Bonnie Spiegel